SLICES OF

Edward Thomas

JANUS PUBLISHING COMPANY
London, England

First published in Great Britain 1993
by Janus Publishing Company

Copyright © Edward Thomas 1993

British Library Cataloguing-in-Publication Data
A catalogue record for this book is available
from the British Library

ISBN 1 85756 032 9

Cover design David Murphy

Phototypeset by Intype, London
Printed and bound in England by
Antony Rowe Ltd, Chippenham, Wiltshire

The characters and situations in this book
are entirely imaginary and bear no relation
to any real person or actual happening.

Contents

A Little Night Relief   1

One in Three   9

Scene Through a Window   15

Total Commitment   19

Coastal Roulette   25
   Henley
   Will
   L.J.
   Greg
   Someone

Essex Persons   67

Going to Extremes   79

Backfire   97

A Little Night Relief

'Damned cold tonight,' said Desmond to himself. 'Must be getting soft. Thought I could take it.'

He tossed and turned under his newspapers. It was a bad time. The vicar who had let him have the back stairs for five winters had moved away. The future and old age lay ahead, he could not sleep, and it was three in the morning. Must do something. He got up from the bench, folded the newspapers and packed them into his battered old briefcase. He climbed to the top of the park railings, had a good look both ways and jumped down. He turned a couple of corners, preparing for the Wimbledon silence to persist for hours yet. But in the distance he could see and hear the silence being broken. There seemed to be a small crowd and cameras, even a couple of powerful lights.

As he came nearer, Desmond could make out about a dozen cameramen and the same number of reporters. There was a limousine parked outside a house and a chauffeur standing by the back passenger door. Desmond spotted a familiar face.

'What's all this in aid of, Johnny?'

Johnny Porter of the *Wimbledon Courier* turned round and was startled to see who was addressing him.

'Hullo, Des. I heard about the vicar moving away. I wondered what was happening to you.'

'A temporary discomfort I assure you, my dear fellow. But what is all this going on at 3.30 in the morning?' Desmond persisted.

'Didn't you know?' replied Johnny. 'This is where Dee Simmons lives.'

'I've heard of her,' Desmond thought hard. 'Isn't she on television?'

1

'That's the one. And this is her big day.'

'But it hasn't started yet,' came the puzzled reply. 'It's hours to dawn. Where's she going? Australia?'

'Don't you read those papers of yours before you get your head under them?' frowned Johnny.

Johnny was a bit fed up with having to be there at all at such an unearthly hour, especially as the story would be emblazoned all over the daily tabloids before his local was published in four days' time. Hardly a scoop.

'National TV is starting its breakfast show at 6.30 this morning. And Dee Simmons is the presenter. They're taking her to the studio in a few minutes.'

'Oh, is that all? And you mean to say you're all here to record the event?'

'Of course,' said the reporter. 'All the TV channels are positioned over there next to the car. It'll be on all the screens on every bulletin today. You might be seen yourself.'

'Not if I can help it,' scoffed the other contemptuously. 'Is this the best they can do, the news gatherers?'

'People will be interested in this,' protested Johnny. 'They'll be excited about the idea of Dee Simmons having to leave her house at 3.30 in the morning.'

'Well, why should that be so special? It's only happening today. Merely one of those – what do you call it – one-off situations?' Desmond was beginning to get impatient with all this.

'Are you kidding?' said the puzzled Johnny. 'She's got this round her neck for a long time. Monday to Friday for the foreseeable future.'

Desmond could feel faint glimmers of interest beginning to percolate through him.

'You mean she's doing this show every weekday?'

'That's right.' Johnny was getting a bit abstracted now. He thought he could hear movements at the front door. 'She's got to be out of the house to be picked up by the limo at this ungodly hour every day. Wouldn't fancy it myself.'

'My goodness, that will be a strain!' whispered Desmond, almost to himself. Then, more loudly, 'I wonder what her husband feels about all this.'

2

Johnny was craning his neck. 'No worries there. She's not married.'

'Not even a boyfriend?' pressed Desmond.

'No one. She's a real loner.'

The gate was opening now and the camera crews moved forward, jostling for position. There were shouts of 'Good morning, Miss Simmons' to which the lady responded.

'How was it, getting up so early?' shouted one.

'Will you be able to keep this up?' said another.

With her usual icy professionalism Dee Simmons parried each facile enquiry. These she was more than accustomed to since they were her own stock-in-trade. She swept into the car combining utmost dignity with determined ordinariness, and the chauffeur drove off slowly enough for the reporters and crews to keep up a jogging pace for a while.

Johnny made a half-hearted attempt to join them and then left it. He hadn't even had the chance to speak to her personally and he was put out about it. The lights were dimmed, sound men packed cases and the company dispersed. Johnny turned back to speak to Desmond again. He was surprised to find the man had disappeared but just as instantly forgot about him; he was very glad to be heading back home on this cold winter night.

'Not even a boyfriend?' pressed Desmond.

'No one. She's a real loner.'

The gate was opening now and as it did so Desmond all but disintegrated into the shadows. He took in a wide sweep of the area and saw that he was not being watched. Of course he wasn't. The focus of attention at that very moment was all too obvious. With utmost stealth he eased back along the hedgerow until he reached the edge of the house. There was a right-of-way and tall trees between the house and Dee Simmons' neighbours. He trod warily along the path until he came to a side door in the fencing. He tried it but it was locked. Moving further along he found that the fencing came to an end and the hedgerow started again. He discovered a hole in it.

Still keeping a careful watch, he scrambled across the lawn and reached the back of the house as the chauffeur-driven car was pulling away at the front. He kept well in against a bush until the reporters had gone and he could no longer hear the slightest sound. Then he began an inspection of the back of the house.

'Louvre windows! Marvellous!' It was more than a whisper and he pulled himself up sharply, even taking another quick look round to see if anyone had heard him. There was a ledge he could stand on and he could reach up easily to a top window to the slats that were so easy to take out. He held his breath in case an alarm went off at the first touch. There was certainly no sign of an announcement of any system on the walls.

He got up on to the ledge and touched the slats of glass. Not a sound. The window was not even locked down firmly from the inside. That was handy. Easy enough to dislodge the slats, but having replaced them afterwards it would be impossible to relock from outside.

He carefully took out the slats and placed them by the ledge. There was ample room for him to climb in.

He found himself in a dining room. With case in hand he made an inspection of the large house. Johnny had said she lived alone. Nonetheless there might be a hidden lover upstairs in one of the rooms so Desmond went to make sure. He was safe.

He came downstairs and went into the enormous lounge. He made a survey of the furniture and set his sights on a most comfortable sofa. He opened his briefcase and took out the newspapers, not to cover himself with, but to lay on the sofa itself. He had not the slightest intention of spoiling the fur-nishings, much less of taking any of them.

He spread the papers out until the sofa was covered and then eased his body onto the soft upholstery.

'God. I haven't had a lie-down on something like this in years,' he murmured.

He did not sleep but it didn't matter. He was content just to lie there in comfort and warmth. The central heating must have been on still for he was not at all cold. The surroundings were new and that kept him on the alert. But it was enough just to be there.

And so he lay still, looking at the ceiling and contented with his new-found fortune. If he was careful he could envisage

long-term possibilities here. The hours passed and he was satis-
fied, with plenty to think about.

As the time approached half past six he thought it would be
quite a novelty to see Miss Simmons making her breakfast
television début. He got up, walked across to the cabinet and
opened the doors. The controls were different from his recollec-
tion of TV sets years before. There were no buttons to switch
to the right, only things to press in. He tried all of them one
by one without success. Realising that the mains were not connected, he went in search of a switch.

He followed the lead from the back of the cabinet until he
found the plug. He switched on and caused an immediate blast
of sound from the set. He raced back to the front of it and tried
frantically to find the volume control. After several fumblings
his fingers touched the right one and he turned the sound down
to nothing. His heart was pounding and he listened, his ears
straining to check whether anyone had heard the racket from
outside. Not a whisper, and he looked down to a silent screen
that was presenting for the very first time the logo of NTV's
earliest-ever transmission. Desmond saw a picture of clouds,
then a sweep down to the Embankment, which he recognised
only too well, and the materialising caption, *The Morning Show*.
The letters in turn dissolved to be reformed into: 'Your hostess:
Dee Simmons'.

Desmond allowed himself a chuckle, for in his case she certainly was, and he carefully brought up the volume in time to
hear her say:

'Good morning and welcome to "The Morning Show".'

She spoke of the months of preparation and how thrilled she
was that this day had finally come.

Desmond settled back on the sofa and for the next hour or
so was bombarded with weather reports, news items, fashion
reports, newspaper reviews, TV programme reviews, all rotat-
ing, one after the other. He began to think he was not missing
very much in not having a television set. Still, his hostess was
letting him have a lot of rest and she was making an efficient
job of linking all these inconsequential items.

She was also providing him with the benefit of watching the
clock which was constantly by her side on the screen. He would
not have to keep diving into his waistcoat pocket for his trusty

5

old watch and chain. He had no idea when the show ended but as long as she was on that screen she could not be at home here.

However, he decided that to be on the safe side he would be well away from the house hours before she returned, and certainly before dawn broke, which these days was about eight o'clock.

At 7.30 he switched Miss Simmons back to oblivion, turned off the main plug and repacked the newspapers into his case. He made sure that everything was as it had been, brushing the sofa, punching the cushions lightly, then he traced his path back to the dining room. Within seconds he was out of the top window and carefully replacing the slats, then through the garden and pausing quietly at the hedge to see if anyone was in the right-of-way. No one was, so he was off.

He was back in the shadows the next morning at 3.30 and once more saw the limousine outside the house. What a difference now, though. Not a sign of anybody else hovering around waiting to take pictures or ask questions. Already Miss Simmons was yesterday's news. She would have to be content with reviewing her own reviews in the slots devoted to Today's Papers in the programme.

Desmond waited until the woman was out of the house and cocooned in the limo which then sleeked off at a much faster rate than it had twenty-four hours earlier.

Then he repeated all the previous day's procedure and was soon settled down on the sofa. Being more relaxed and feeling almost at home he now fell asleep immediately and enjoyed three hours of unconsciousness. He woke up at 6.30 to switch on and see what his hostess was doing, went back to sleep again and even chanced staying a bit longer before leaving the house.

His subsequent nights grew into a pattern. The weather was becoming steadily colder and he was thankful to leave the bitterness of the park at the worst time of the night to take warm refuge for a few hours. He came to dread the weekends, for his hostess did not work then and the cold nights had to be soldiered through in their entirety.

On the Wednesday of the fourth week the night air was particularly vicious. Desmond made his way as usual to the house but was surprised to see no limousine there. He checked his pocket watch and saw that he was slightly later than usual. He decided the car must have left a few minutes earlier. Nonetheless he went through the motions with perhaps a shade more vigilance. All was deadly silent, though, and he settled down on the sofa; but the house seemed colder and he could not sleep very well. At 6.28 he switched on the television and listened to the music running up to transmission time.

At 6.30 the programme's logo appeared, followed immediately by the face of the presenter. Almost as an afterthought Desmond said to himself:

'Oh, she's not on this morning.'

Immediately he thought it he shot up into a sitting position. The presenter introduced the newsreader who began his first story.

'And *we* make the main news today. Public attention has focused on the National Television Company following the dismissal of Dee Simmons yesterday from *The Morning Show* because of alleged poor ratings.'

Desmond froze. But he did not hear any more of the newsreader's words as his eyes and ears were suddenly diverted to the sitting-room door which was opening slowly.

One in Three

She told him it was the last time he would ever cause trouble again in the family. He backed away in disbelief holding up his hands in a vain attempt to shield himself. But the trigger was pulled and down he went. As he dropped down behind the sofa at the back of the stage he was well hidden and did not bother with a blood capsule. Nobody would have noticed the effect.

Sheila raced off the stage with the gun and placed it on the props table. Then she went back to the dressing room for another chat with Maureen, the wardrobe co-ordinator.

'That's me finished now till the curtain,' said Sheila to Maureen who was browsing through some designs for the next show. 'I'll be glad when this one's over tomorrow. I've been so tired this week, getting home, tearing down here every night. I think it's getting both of us down.'

'It shouldn't be so bad for Brian,' laughed Maureen, 'tucked behind that sofa for nearly a whole act. He can catch up on some sleep then.'

Sheila said he could never do that as he always concentrated on the action so much. Though his character was dead from then on, it was still the centre of attention while the others of the family spent the rest of the play trying to work out how to cover up the murder they knew a sister had committed. Brian said that some of them were still shaky on their lines for those final scenes, not that he could do a thing to help any of them, but it just put him constantly on edge.

'Why do you both carry on with all this if it's such an effort?' Maureen asked.

Sheila reckoned neither of them would for much longer. She and Brian had been involved in almost every show since they were married and it was taking its toll. She had told Maureen before how the last eight years had been a mixture. Now she felt it was getting worse and it frustrated her not to be able to pinpoint it, because she still felt so much love for him.

'Don't you ever talk about it?' asked Maureen. Sheila shook her head in such a way that Maureen got the impression discussion of the topic was over for the moment. So instead she asked Sheila for her opinion about the designs she had worked on for the next show. Sheila brushed off her tiredness and depression and showed genuine interest. In fact she was still absorbed when the assistant stage manager knocked on the door and told her the police were just going on. That was her cue to get ready for curtain call so she left Maureen and went to the side of the stage. Moments later the curtain came down, Sheila walked on and joined Brian who was just getting up and they took a curtain call with the others.

Afterwards in the bar Sheila was even more conscious than ever of Brian's detachment from her. He spent the whole time he was there chatting up a new girl to the company, a beautiful young woman. As Sheila stood there, glass in hand, not paying attention to the conversation going on in the group around her, a sense of panic began to take over. Her sense of security had been slowly chipping away over the last year and now it appeared to have gone. The searing possessiveness in her was starting to make her sweat as she watched them talking and laughing together. Exaggeration flooded her mind as she thought of those extra rehearsals they had needed together. They had spent hours working on that difficult first act. She felt sick and knew she would have to make a huge effort. She broke away from her group and walked across to Brian and the new girl, not giving a hint of the screaming going on inside.

All three smiled broadly at each other as Brian said without forcing it: 'Ready to go then?'

Not a word was exchanged in the car. As Brian was locking the garage door Sheila was already making coffee. She didn't usually when they were late but the coffee was a sign of a burning to talk rather than of thirst. Brian sensed it too when he came in. He mumbled something about it making a change and she said yes.

They sat down and started drinking. After only a couple of sips she put her cup down.

'I want to know what's going on.'

It threw him completely. She was never as direct as this. He looked awkward and did not answer straightaway but sat gazing at her unhappy face. Finally:

'You know already, don't you?'

She nodded and held off the tears no longer. Then she was on her feet screaming: 'You bastard' and over to the settee swiping him before he could collect himself. He managed to get up and restrain her. He begged her to calm down and sit with him on the settee so they could talk.

Then it happened, the conversation she had dreaded but had seen coming for a long time. It was all following the pattern she knew it would. They had been drifting a long time, hadn't they? He reminded her of the bad holiday they'd had, how they had vowed they would not go away again together, not just the two of them. Well, that wasn't right, was it, for a married couple to be that fed up with each other? It was all predictable. He had not wanted to hurt her but he could not help himself. Oh, sure. Everybody said that these days. Yes, he had been having an affair with the new girl in the company for six weeks.

She could not bring herself to ask him what he was going to do. She could not stand hearing him say he was going to leave, not yet anyway, it was bound to come to it soon enough, but she did not want to think about it yet. She went through the motions of insisting on her sleeping in the other room rather than his doing so. Throughout the monotonous hours of the night she thought of the irony of 'sleeping'. It was the last thing she could do.

The next morning she left a note saying she probably would not see him before the theatre that night. And she didn't. She wandered about all day, combing the streets and the parks trying to sort out the madness brewing in her mind. She went over and over their chequered marriage until she thought herself into a state of numbness. She took on a sense of unreality. As she looked at other people going about their business she began to consider seriously that this horror was not happening to her. It couldn't be. It was all reserved for some unfortunate being beside her. Her head began to glaze over. She started feeling dizzy. She would have to stop. She had to get through this day somehow. There was the performance. She would have to survive that if nothing else.

Making a supreme effort she walked into the theatre and into the dressing room. She was the first one there. She took her time getting ready. The others arrived one by one and gradually she became relaxed as she immersed herself in the character she was portraying. She even managed to be natural with the new girl when she came in. She did not know whether Brian had got in touch with her to tell her what had happened the night before. She found herself too exhausted on that score to care. The hatred she had built up during the day was for Brian.

And so the performance began. Sheila started the play off so she was in position a good ten minutes before the curtain went up. She still had not seen Brian and realised now that the first time she would see him would be on the stage. She preferred it that way. The curtain went up and they were off. Strangely her lines seemed sharper to her now than at any time. Came the point when Brian arrived and they had a scene together. When their eyes met nothing showed. They were both determined to be absorbed in their parts.

One interval came and went. Then Act Two. It was going well. Sheila came off for the second interval and helped herself to a cup of coffee from the cast's tray. She was feeling very calm now and there was still no sign of Brian backstage. That was good. It helped her to relax more. The call came for beginners for Act Three. She went out to the wings to be handed the gun by the assistant stage manager. There was only a brief time in hand but she said to the others she was just going to the lavatory. One or two thought that odd as she did not usually cut it that fine.

She was back in time and on for the final act. She went through the dialogue with Brian as usual. Their voices rose. She told him it was the last time he would ever cause trouble again in the family. He backed away in disbelief holding up his hands in a vain attempt to shield himself. But the trigger was pulled and down he went. He dropped down behind the sofa at the back of the stage. Sheila raced off the stage with the gun and placed it on the props table.

Twenty-five minutes later Maureen looked at her watch in the dressing room and heard the policemen going on. She had not seen Sheila so she wandered out as the ASM was checking the cast for the curtain call. He asked her if she had seen Sheila.

When Maureen said no they both started looking for her. It was time for the curtain and the stage manager said angrily that they would have to go ahead without her. The curtain fell and the applause began. Everyone went into line, heard the whisper that Sheila was not around, and waited for Brian to get up from behind the sofa.

Scene Through a Window

It seemed odd to her that people still felt sorry for her. As she eased the brake off the wheelchair and manoeuvred it towards the window, she thought of a line from the play she had seen with Charles the previous evening.

'It's stupid to talk like that', Mrs Whyte had declared in *Waters of the Moon*. 'Life isn't fair or unfair or comic or tragic or anything else. Life is life. One must just accept it.'

Muriel thought that was quite right. She guided the chair into her favourite position by the window. She could hear Charles cleaning his teeth in the bathroom.

It was a beautiful summer morning as she looked down on the garden. The swimming pool already looked inviting. She would take a dip in it later in the day when Mavis came round to help her. Her eyes travelled to the right of the pool and alighted on the magnificent display of flowers Mavis was so expert at tending.

A touch of annoyance seeped in as she considered that from the time it had happened, gardening had become something she could not continue. How she had always loved dealing with the garden.

'Right, darling, I'm off now.'

Charles' voice shook her out of her moment of self-pity and she felt annoyed again for falling into the trap. She looked up at Charles and smiled as he bent down to kiss her.

'You'll be back for lunch?' Muriel asked.

'Oh, yes. I'm only visiting the one factory. Then there's the reception in the Mayor's Parlour. Should be home by one o'clock.'

'I hope you'll find me in the pool by then.'

'I hope so too,' he said as he squeezed her hand. 'Bye now.'

She heard his footsteps descend the stairs and noted that for once he did not protest about her staying upstairs. He always thought it was safer for her to be on the ground floor, which it probably was, but she was determined not to miss this glorious view on summer mornings. Plenty of time to go downstairs later with Mavis' help.

The summer. When it was a good one, there was nothing to match it in England. All this, the grounds of this lovely old house in the country which Charles had been able to buy; she would not part with it. And how good it was that Charles could share in it in the long summer recess. Parliament would not be sitting now until after the Party Conference in October.

The Party Conference. As she looked out on the garden and the swimming pool, her mind went back to it again. She couldn't help it. It was still less than two years ago. The middle of the night in Llandudno. She heard again the fearsome explosion that woke her up and she found herself travelling downwards. When she came to rest amidst the screams and rubble, there was no sign of Charles. She had felt the momentary stab of pain as the great piece of stone seemed to bury itself in her back and then she passed out.

Muriel shook herself and sighed. Her eyes travelled leftwards to the garage and the car standing in front of it. Once again she felt annoyance with Charles. So often he did not put the car away. He really ought to. The security people had pointed it out often enough.

Muriel could hear Charles speaking on the telephone. It had rung just as he'd reached the stairs. She sighed again. That bloody bomb had put her in a wheelchair and now she could not see to her own flowers anymore. Never mind. What was it Wintherhalter had said in the play last night? 'The human animal is very adaptable'. Thank God for that.

But not many complaints really, thought Muriel, as she reflected on the swimming pool, which was a boon, and her piano-playing. What a lifesaver that had proved; which reminded her, she must work on that today. She was taking part in a charity concert the following month.

Then there was Charles. Dear Charles. He was devoted to her. He had come to terms with the idea of no longer being able to decide on anything spontaneously. Everything required

16

planning. But that was his strength. An expert organiser, who organised so much for her. They had been to the theatre the previous night. They went most weeks when he was home.

She looked up as the whirr of a helicopter circled overhead before racing out over the country. The birds heightened their song.

Yes, that was the main drawback. No more spontaneity. That and the winters, which were still so difficult. Charles tried to get home as often as possible, but the long night sessions in the House ruled it out sometimes. But that went with the job, with being the wife of an MP.

Her mind half on next month's concert, Muriel looked down at the garage, thinking it could do with repainting. She heard Charles replace the receiver and close the door behind him. She opened her window, deciding to tell him now about the garage woodwork in case she forgot later.

He looked up as he always did and smiled. She called out:

'We must do something about the paintwork on the garage.'

He looked at it and called up in agreement. 'I'll see to it at the weekend.'

'And why is the car outside again?'

'Oh, you know how it is. We were so late getting back last night.' He laughed.

She gave him a look of mock annoyance and he blew her a kiss. She blew him one back and closed the window. She watched as he found his car key and opened the door. He sat in the seat and switched on the engine.

Just as at Llandudno, her consciousness left her momentarily as the explosion rent the air. Trees shook off leaves, the birds scattered and her window rattled. The dust cleared and her eyes settled on the area next to the garage. Motionless. Nothing happening. Standstill time. If only it could remain so. Two full seconds passed before Muriel let out her tormented scream. She clawed at the latch but now the window would not budge.

She looked at the wreck. The roof of the car had become a gable. Two doors were wide open, one of them almost off its hinges. Metal was strewn everywhere. She could just make out Charles' head slumped forward over the steering wheel. When she saw his severed right arm lying on the ground by the door, she nearly vomited through her screams.

'Please, God, let him be dead, now,' she quavered as her hands went to the telephone by her side. She made a supreme effort to keep herself still as she started to press the numbers. She did not need to. She heard shouts and cries and a police siren way out in the distance. The neighbours had got there first. Her eyes went back to the window.

A man, old Mr Skinner, was hurrying over to the car. His wife, close behind, screamed at him.

'Don't get too close. There might be another one to go off.'

'I've got to get to him.' Muriel heard the elderly man protest. She saw him reach the driver's seat and touch Charles' shoulder. She saw Mr Skinner wince. Then she saw him look up at her sitting agonised at the window. He shook his head at her and, just for a moment, Muriel relaxed.

Total Commitment

Fred fixed his cap with a sharp movement as the customer came running up the station approach towards him. The man looked contrite.

'Morning, Mr Johnson,' said Fred, 'you're so late you'll have to gulp down your tea quickly.' He handed the cup to the man who scarcely had any breath in him.

'I . . . I don't think I want it this morning, thank you, Fred.' There was a quiver in Mr Johnson's voice.

Fred's eyes opened wide. 'You *know* I make a pot at 6.52 exactly. Just enough for the six of you. It's a waste of tea if one of you doesn't drink it. Now come along into the waiting room.'

Mr Johnson knew it was no good. Still gasping and clutching his briefcase, he took the cup, went in and looked at the other five as he sat down. Sympathy showed for him in their faces.

Fred saw a casual approaching and went into the ticket office that joined the waiting room. A casual was not a season ticket holder. There would be no tea for her. She asked for a return to London and was quickly through the other door onto the platform. She caught a glimpse of the tea drinkers first and looked puzzled.

Fred emerged from the ticket office just as Harry Forbes put his cup down.

'Well, Fred, getting nearer each day. What the devil are you going to do without this station to look after?'

'Can't even think about it, Mr Forbes. Not looking forward to it after thirty-five years.'

'There's a lot you could do,' chimed in Miss Harrison. She was thinking about retirement herself. 'I'm so looking forward to being able to stay in the village on lovely summer mornings like this. Not getting up so early. I'll be able to spend the whole time on my garden.'

Fred shrugged. 'I keep mine up to scratch every day. Only takes an hour when I get home in the afternoon.'

He collected the empty cups and took them into the ticket office to place them in the small sink. He came back and checked his watch. It was 7.06.

'Time to go, ladies and gentlemen.

The customers stood up in unison. Mr Johnson was still gulping his tea. When he got to his feet he put the still half-full cup on the table.

Fred looked heavenward. Johnson was a new season ticket holder of only three weeks' standing. Fred still had not licked him into shape. He led his troop out through the doors onto the platform, marched them the short distance to the end of it, down onto the track and across to the up-line platform.

This was part of his service for the season ticket holders who caught the only train that stopped at his station for London. In this way they did not have to clamber over the footbridge. It was a major event of the day. They marched in single file behind their Pied Piper.

Four minutes later they watched as the train entered from one of the two tracks that converged on the station in a V shape from the east.

Fred opened the usual door and all six got in, bidding Fred a good day. There was no choice in the matter, no question of the six spreading themselves along the platform and selecting their own carriages. The one casual customer, not part of the charmed circle, surveyed the scene somewhat bemused before boarding.

Fred closed the carriage door and with great ceremony sig-nalled to the guard that the train could leave. His line of vision followed the train until it was completely out of sight before he moved an inch.

Then he followed his routine with cutting-edge precision. He left the platform down the ramp to his car park. It was truly his. The parish council had given him permission to clear the patch of waste ground nobody had claimed, which he had carefully laid to tarmac. Then he had painted four white lines on each side to establish ten parking spaces. These should be ample for season ticket holders for years to come.

He took out his notebook to check the car numbers. He could easily have seen the five vehicles from the platform but his ritual was to visit his car park immediately after the departure of the direct London train. Then he would place a tick against each registration number in his book.

He checked for cracks in the tarmac because the weather was warming up. He looked up at the blue sky and concluded it was going to be a scorcher of a day. He looked at his beloved car park and re-crossed the line to sort out the waiting room. He tut-tutted as he surveyed the scene. Some of his customers were getting sloppy. Probably Mr Forbes, who was passing his bad influence on to Mr Johnson.

Fred was not in the habit of selling newspapers in the waiting room, but he took in all the freesheets and leaflets he could find. These could range from local newspapers to the Tesco Times. The left side of the table was devoted to British Rail publications. BR News was included and no customer was ever deprived of the regular message from the Chairman. On the right were other journals and information. If the elderly Miss Harrison wanted to find out about ski-ing trips in the Cairngorms, there was no need for her to consult Thomas Cook's.

Fred went about rearranging his table, positioning all the literature available with a frightening orderliness. He spent a good fifteen minutes creating patterns, checking and re-checking for symmetry. At last the task was complete, until the next customer would come in and browse over it all. He shuddered at the thought.

Next there were the six cups to be washed and the teapot to be emptied. He returned to his ticket office and recalled young Johnson's impertinence at trying to get out of drinking his tea. The very idea!

Ten minutes later the cups and saucers were back in the cupboard and the tea towel carefully folded over the bar Fred had put up on the wall.

Now for the hour on the platform garden. He took from another cupboard his trowel, rake and small bucket for weed collection and headed out along the down-line platform. He approached the brick and concrete structure built some ten years before to house the earth and plants he had tended ever since. He looked wistfully across to the other platform as he always did. Yet again he bemoaned the fact that he had not been able to create a flower bed for the up-line platform because it was narrower. He sighed and set about his work.

Fifty minutes later the garden was a picture once more. He was especially proud of the herbaceous border which needed constant attention if it was to look exactly the same all the way round.

Fred gathered all the garden implements and took them back to the cupboard in the ticket office.

A young woman was waiting to buy the ticket she bought three times a week.

Fred looked at his watch. 'You're early for the 8.45.'

'Yes,' she said. 'It was such a lovely morning I decided to come out earlier.'

Fred deposited the garden things and issued her with a ticket. He walked out onto the platform with her.

'How are you getting on at the big house?' he asked.

'Oh, fine. Lady Parker is good to work for.'

He nodded and pottered about until the local train came in and the woman got on.

As soon as the train was out of the way, Fred took out his notebook to record his daily observations about the flowers he had just seen to.

His next move was to stir up some white paint. Some of the wood on the open shelter on the up-line platform had been annoying him for days. So he collected paint pot, brush and ladder and crossed the line once more. He took his jacket off as it was now very hot, but he kept his cap on. Just as he was climbing up to reach the offending woodwork, a sound caught his attention. He looked round the side of the open shelter, incredulous. Someone was driving into his car park.

He raced down the ladder, replaced the paint pot lid, put his jacket on and dashed as hard as he could out to the car park. The woman was just getting out of the car.

'Hey, what do you think you are doing?' Fred shouted as he ran.

The woman looked startled and confused. 'What does it look like?' she had the effrontery to ask.

Fred could scarcely contain himself. 'You can't park *here*!' he said, as though she had driven into Buckingham Palace.

'What are you talking about?' she said. 'It's a car park.'

'It's for season ticket holders only,' Fred snorted.

The woman blinked. 'How many more are there to come?'

'None,' came the reply. 'They all leave on the 7.10.'

The woman looked round. 'But you've only got five cars here. There are five spaces left.'

'That's beside the point.'

'I don't believe this,' said the woman. 'You've got space here and you won't let me park?'

'Very sorry, madam,' said Fred with great pomp. 'It's the thin end of the wedge. If I let you park, anybody might try the same thing. Then I might get another season ticket application, and the whole thing'll get out of hand.'

'Well, where else can I park?' said the woman in exasperation.

'There are spaces beside the pub down the road.'

The woman looked at her watch. 'But I might miss the train. I've got to get the connection at Ketchworth.'

Fred pursed his lips and looked at his watch. 'The 9.30, yes. You might miss it, but I'm very sorry, madam. There's nothing I can do about it.'

The woman could not be bothered to argue further. She got into her car and drove off at an angry speed.

Fred, also angry, marched back onto the platform, still unable to believe that someone could contravene his wishes about the car park, his car park. Dammit, hadn't he spent hours creating the magnificent notice at the entrance declaring for whom the car park was designated?

He was so out of sorts he decided not to return to the painting of the shelter until after the 9.30 had gone. Instead, he spent the five remaining minutes reflecting on people's attitudes today.

He was still standing at the platform edge ruminating when he heard the familiar sounds in the distance. This was the one time of the day when two trains converged together at the V just before the station. The local train stopped of course at the junction to let the fast from Shellerton to London through.

Fred continued thinking about the insolence of the young

woman as his eyes searched to the right for the two trains to appear. He spotted them almost simultaneously from either side of the thick woodland separating the two tracks. They came steadily nearer and Fred thought that the local was going faster than usual. It ought to be slowing down soon.

The thought was overtaken by the realisation that the driver was not going to stop until he reached the station. There must be something wrong with the signals.

Fred backed away, sweat breaking out. It was really happening. The local train carried on and was ahead of the fast. The driver was nearly into the station before his colleague in the fast saw what was happening. He slammed on the brakes but it was too late.

The local train was pushed onto the down line and several carriages began buckling and cascading onto the platform opposite to where Fred was standing open-mouthed. He was near the other end of the platform, and the shunted train came to a forlorn stop just past him.

Fred scrambled down onto the line, raced round the front of the train and up onto the platform. He passed along the wreckage and saw an outstretched hand reaching up from a horizontal carriage window. He ignored it. He was totally oblivious of the beseeching hand and of the surprise on the face of its possessor. He rushed past the twisted metal, the imploring cries and the ominous smell of something scorching.

'Oh, my chrysanths!' he cried. 'Just look at 'em . . . my chrysanths!'

Coastal Roulette

Four men were in Eastbourne
on Sunday, 15 April.
The wheel began spinning,
all the way up to Beachy Head.
It picked a number . . .

HENLEY

'I'm going to kill myself when I get back.'

'Oh, yes?'

'Don't you believe me?'

'Henley, I know you're devastated about not winning. But you're in pretty august company. Just think for a moment. The Academy Awards have been going for sixty years. That's three times sixty actors who've lost. They've had to. You couldn't have one winner out of four nominees, otherwise.'

Well done, Lester. Ever the practical one. His mathematical mind has been a godsend in my career, thought Henley. Being rational didn't help though. Not in the end.

'I wanted that Oscar, Les. I wanted it.'

'Of course you bloody did. Anyone who's nominated for it wants it desperately. I felt bad about it too last night, even though I didn't think you stood a chance.'

Henley was visibly pained and surprised. 'Why not?'

'Didn't think it was possible, not up against de Niro tearing his heart out in that AIDS drama. Too much social comment in it they all agreed with.'

'Well, why didn't you tell me at the start?' asked Henley, sinking into more depression.

'I've known you too long,' answered Lester. 'It's taken me five years as your manager to get to know your moods. If I'd said before you didn't stand a chance, you wouldn't have bothered to come here on the way home.'

'So what?'

'Question of good form. The Academy likes the nominees to be at the ceremony. Looks so much better to see the vulnerable live face when the names are rolled out, instead of a still picture on the screen. Good publicity too. Today's Tuesday. The show goes out on ITV tonight. All the folks back home will see you on the box. Another Brit making good in Hollywood. It's all valuable. They'll feel sorry for you too. We shan't get back in time for it, though.'

'Thank God for that.'

'We are in a gloomy state today,' sighed Lester. 'Come on. We'd better get going for the airport. Are you nearly packed?'

'Not quite,' said Henley. 'How long have we got?' His voice was getting edgy.

'No immediate rush. I've ordered the taxi for three o'clock. We've got about an hour till then.'

'That's no time,' snapped Henley. 'It'll go in a flash.' There was a sudden silence between them. Lester stopped collecting up the papers he was putting into a briefcase.

'Oh, God. I'm sorry, Les. You're the last person I want to take it out on.'

Lester smiled and looked awkward. He never knew how to take compliments or apologies. His was a clear mathematical mind, but he couldn't understand the outburst.

'You *are* wound up about this, aren't you?' he observed. 'Let me order a couple of stiff whiskies before we embark on this foul journey.'

'If you like.' Henley's reply was unenthusiastic. Lester picked up the telephone and spoke to Room Service. When he replaced the receiver, he found Henley ready to talk again.

'The Oscar is only a part of it, the last part in fact.'

His face clouded over. The lines showed prominently in his forehead. He hesitated. Lester tried to look encouraging.

'It's what you just said,' continued Henley, 'about the time.'

26

'Well, what about it?' There was an awkward half-laugh in Lester's voice.

'That's one of the things that grinds into me all the time, the passage of time.'

There was another pause and Lester looked confused. 'Sorry, Henley, I'm not with you.'

Henley took a deep breath. 'I've never gone into this with you before. It's all part of the reason why I go to the chap in Harley Street every so often.'

'But you've always treated that as a joke,' said Lester. 'When I asked you about it once, you laughed it off. Said something about it being fashionable for stars to go for analysis. I never asked about it again.'

'It never was a joke, Lester. It was a defence mechanism to make light of it. I've been seeing him for years. Long before I met up with you I used to see him, not as I do now, half a dozen times every year. I saw him once a week at Bart's, on the NHS. Couldn't afford Harley Street in those days.'

This was all news to Lester. 'How long have you been seeing him then?'

'I first went to Turnbull fifteen years ago.'

'When you were twenty?'

'Yes.'

'Bloody hell, Henley,' exclaimed his manager. 'That was a good ten years before I met you. I thought you only started going to him when the big money began rolling in.'

'Oh, no. It was only then that I transferred to his private practice.'

'Well, what was the trouble? What *is* the trouble?' Lester was beginning to be concerned.

Henley started sweating. He had never voiced it to anyone before except his doctor. 'The Oscars ceremony. It seemed as though it all flashed by in five minutes.'

'So?'

'It's screwing me up – the thought of it.'

Lester was even more confused. 'I'm not following this. You're worried because that junket didn't seem to last long?'

Henley nodded his head.

'Well, I only wish I felt like that. The bloody thing started at half past five and didn't end till nearly eleven. And it felt like it to me.'

'Then you don't know how lucky you are,' was the response, measured and serious. Lester gaped at him. 'What's so terrible about time going quickly? It means you've enjoyed yourself.'

'That's where you are wrong, Lester. There's no enjoyment in studying your watch, seeing the seconds and minutes ticking away, staring at them until your face breaks into a sweat.'

Lester sat down to face him. 'Is that what *you* do?'

'I did. Fifteen years ago. That's what first sent me off to Turnbull. I'm what is called an obsessional neurotic.'

Lester wanted to help, but it was all alien to him. 'What does it mean?'

Henley sighed defeatedly. 'It means I fix my mind on certain things and cannot let them go. Believe me, when time goes quickly, it's not because I've enjoyed myself. I came out of the Chandler Pavilion last night sweating like a pig. It was 11.02 exactly. I felt I'd only gone in there half an hour before. I felt sick.'

Lester frowned. 'Is it always like that?

'Sometimes there's peace. If I calm down, or when I go to bed. I relax then.' Unhappiness and self-pity were creeping up on him by the second. 'Sonia couldn't handle it. That's really why she left.'

'She might have come out here on this trip, though,' said Lester, mildly embittered.

'You couldn't blame her. All my differing moods. She wasn't up to understanding. Nor was Stella. Everyone said it was Sonia who broke us up. Funny when you think about it. Stella tried to warn her about the neurosis. Poor Sonia didn't have the sense to listen. Perhaps if I'd been able to talk to one of them about what the matter really was . . .'

The knock at the door signalled the arrival of the whiskies. The waiter was quickly in and out delivering the order. Henley got up and packed the last few things into a holdall. He took the glass Lester offered him and stood by the window looking out at the smoggy day.

'So you never enjoy anything?' said Lester. 'You never stop thinking about the clock?'

'That's about it,' came the unhappy reply. 'I can hardly ever think about the thing I'm doing, only the time it's taking to do it.'

'This neurosis, what did you call it?'

'Obsessional.'

'Obsessional. Does it take other forms?'

'Oh, yes. What I've told you is only the half of it. Can't tell you what it did to me when I reached my thirty-fifth a couple of months ago. It was a nightmare, that party.'

Lester interjected. 'But we had a great time that night. You and Sonia and all of us.'

'Yes, I needed all my acting ability to get through it. But my mind was on the horror of it all. Over and over I kept thinking about one thing. That line of Joanne Woodward's in *Rachel, Rachel* when she reached the same age. She said: 'This is my last ascending summer'. Do you remember it?'

'No,' said Lester, somewhat lost.

'At least when I'm obsessed with my age, I'm not thinking about the passage of time. When one idea takes a firm hold, all the rest falls away. That's what this neurosis does to you.'

Lester was baffled. 'What about Turnbull? You've been seeing him all these years.'

'He does his best,' said Henley. 'He said it was like a tap that turns on and off when the obsessions come and go. But they still don't know what turns the tap off. They're still searching.'

The telephone buzzed. Lester thanked reception and said they would be down straightaway. No, it was all right. They didn't need any help. Wearily Henley picked up his holdall, they finished their whiskies, and made their way down to the lobby.

The hotel manager beamed as the photographers did their work and he told them of the pleasure it had been to have such a worthy nominee staying there. He bade them have a nice day. Henley wanted to tell him there was no hope of that. But he smiled and shook hands.

The taxi driver knew whom he was taking to the airport. He had a bit of notepaper and a pen ready. He thrust both into Henley's hands.

'If you don't mind. To my daughter, Chantal. She's crazy about you.'

'Of course,' said Henley and duly obliged.

When they were settled in the cab, Lester returned to the subject. 'Turnbull may have done his best. But perhaps that's not been good enough. Have you thought of trying somebody, or something, else?'

'I've had it, Les,' answered Henley. 'I've got used to him after all these years. I can tell him anything. Already have done, no end of stuff from the darkest recesses of the mind. I would have to dredge it all up again with someone new. I couldn't face it again.'

Lester looked at him as they speeded to Los Angeles Airport and thought he had never seen Henley looking so unhappy.

'What are you going to do then?'

'I told you. I'm going to kill myself.'

The taxi driver looked in his mirror quickly. Lester shifted uncomfortably.

'Keep your voice down, Henley. And for Heaven's sake, don't start all that again.'

'I'm serious, Lester. George Sanders made a vow quite rationally that when he was sixty-five he would commit suicide. And he did.'

'You're not telling me that you've had your mind made up for years to do the same?' Lester tried to speak softly as he could see the taxi driver was bursting with interest.

'No, not years, only since my birthday. I was already nominated. I decided if I didn't win, that was it. I was going to chuck it all.'

'So how are you going to do it?' Lester's concern for his client was beginning to be overtaken by a feeling of awkwardness. All this conversation was taking place within the earshot of the taxi driver.

'Can't you come to Tenerife with me? It's only a few days.'

Lester was almost relieved that Henley appeared to be changing the subject.

'Wish I could. But I must be in London for a conference on Thursday.'

'Pity. I'd have liked you to be with me in my last days.'

Lester did feel some relief now. Henley was getting back to his maudlin self.

'Oh, yes? What's going to happen at the end of them?'

'You don't believe me, do you? Well, I'll tell you. The plane arrives from Tenerife on Sunday at Gatwick. It's only a short hop from there on the train to Eastbourne.'

'Eastbourne?' said Lester. 'You haven't been there for years!'

'That's right,' answered Henley. 'Not since I was a kid. I want to see some old haunts. See how it's changed. I also want to see the place where Stella had such a big hit last summer.'

'The Congress?' queried Lester.

'That's the one. They were building the place as we moved away. I've never seen it.'

'Well, why now suddenly? What do you want to go back for while you're in this mood?'

Henley developed a glazed look. 'I've worked it out, Les. I can remember the route as though it was only yesterday. Up the length of Carlisle Road to the start of the Downs, then across to Beachy Head; the highest cliff in England.'

'And that's where you're going to do it?' asked Lester. 'That's where you're going to end it all?'

'That's it.' Henley appeared to be wrapping up the conversation.

Lester was uneasy. This was not the first time Henley had spoken of death. He was inclined not to take it too seriously. On the other hand Henley had never spoken of it before so matter-of-factly. It was all much more planned and detailed this time. Yet why was he telling him his plans in such detail?

His mind was taken off the matter as he felt the taxi swerving off the road into a service station. As the driver got out, Lester saw that the man wanted to speak to him.

'I'm just going to get something from the service shop,' said Lester.

Henley nodded.

Lester got out of the car and signalled to the driver to meet him at the shop. The driver filled the tank, walked to the shop and paid the bill. Out of sight of Henley, he spoke to Lester.

'What is all this? Mr Beaufort is going to kill himself?'

Lester laughed, too loudly, brushing it aside. 'Oh, don't take any notice of that.' He slapped a hand on the man's shoulder. 'You know what actors are like,' he said quietly. The driver was thrilled to be taken into the manager's confidence. 'The ones who always talk of suicide are never the ones who do it.' He roared with laughter.

The taxi driver laughed too. 'If you say so,' he said, reassured.

'Now go back to the car before me,' Lester said to the man. 'We don't want Mr Beaufort thinking we've been talking about him, do we?'

'No, of course not,' answered his delighted conspirator, who walked across the forecourt. Moments later, Lester followed.

A few days later, Henley was in Eastbourne. There was much activity around the Congress Theatre. They were getting ready for a Royal Variety Performance. Princess Margaret would be coming that Sunday night.

Henley looked at the posters advertising the event: Danny La Rue, Tom O'Connor, Dai Francis, Anckorn and Dolovich. He sighed; a typical show biz bill. They might have invited Stella to appear. Since her summer success there last year, she had become one of Britain's top comediennes.

He laughed momentarily. Stella: yes, she was a funny lady. She liked Lester too, always got on well with him. And what a good sort *he* was. A grim smile covered Henley's face. He felt sure he'd put Lester off the scent by being so truthful about his intentions for this day.

He turned away from the Congress. People were already nudging each other. 'Don't look now, but do you see who that is over there?'

Carlisle Road stretched away from the theatre up to the South Downs and eventually on to Beachy Head. Henley set off slowly, tired and depressed.

WILL

'Look this way, Mrs Forbes.'

'Can you take your hat off a moment.'

'Hold up the walking boots.'

The instructions seemed endless. Will and Joan Forbes were still smiling but their grins appeared to be getting more fixed. At last the photographers were finished. An enthusiastic young woman came up to them.

'That's fine, Mr Forbes. Now you know the arrangement. We'll meet you at Birling Gap around two o'clock, if that's all right.'

'We'll try and get there by then,' replied Will. 'The train gets in at 11.10. We'll have an early lunch, then it'll take two hours or so to walk to the Gap. See you in the hotel.'

'Fine,' said the woman.

'Come along now, please,' urged an irate guard. 'We've held the train up five minutes already.'

'We've finished now,' came the reply.

Joan Forbes had already stepped into the first-class compartment as her husband waved goodbye and the train pulled out of Victoria.

'I don't know why we can't be left alone on a day like this,' she said as Will joined her and closed the door.

'You know how it is,' he replied. 'Publicity is always good.'

'I don't exactly call *Rambler and Fell Walker Magazine* publicity,' said the irritated Joan.

'Don't agree at all. Not a bad idea for an MP to help promote one of the more healthy pursuits of our society: outdoor life and all that.'

'God, you are pompous at times.'

Will had given up showing annoyance even if he still felt it. 'Well anyway, it won't take long, once we meet up with them again. A quick couple of pictures at Crowlink, then it's all over.'

'This is one day I look forward to every year. A couple of hours walking over the Downs along the south coast. It recharges the batteries. I prefer it to the club walking any day. All those squawking W.I. types, constantly yapping on when you want to look at the scenery.'

'Yes, I know, Joan. But I really think if we can encourage others to do something healthy like this, we should.'

Joan sighed and looked out at the dreariness of south London. Soon the train was pulling in to Clapham Junction. A couple of yobbos slid into their compartment. Joan looked at her husband as they planted their muddy shoes on the upholstery opposite them. Will was bursting to tell them of it, but he knew that as a public figure he did not want to make a scene. Joan recognised this and looked away disdainfully.

Two hours later they were on the seafront at Eastbourne. It was windy, the middle of April. Easter had come and gone, so there weren't many people about. They both took in the gulps of air they could not get in London, and strolled up the slope to the Wish Tower restaurant. Joan found a secluded corner facing the sea and cliffs while Will purchased two coffees and was recognised. There was laughter.

They had not spoken much on the train. Now the invigorating air had given Joan back her enthusiasm.

'What was that all about?' she asked as he placed the coffees and cake on the table.

'They just said they'd seen *Question Time* on Thursday. They felt sorry for the way Sir Robin had treated me.'

'That was your fault, letting him get away with it,' said Joan bitterly.

'He was most apologetic,' said Will. 'And I understood. It was near the end of the programme. He would have cut any of us short, whoever had been talking.'

'Yes, and it just had to be you, didn't it?'

'Drink your coffee, Joan, before it gets cold.'

'Don't bloody patronise me.'

Will looked round quickly. There was nobody within earshot. He sipped his coffee.

'How did it all go wrong?' Joan suddenly cried. 'What have you got to show for it now?'

There was a pause before Will said: 'Pride.'

Joan gave an ironic laugh. 'Oh yes, pride. Not sure what I've got then. I slogged my guts out for you for ten years building up your safe seat. Then you had to chuck it away.'

'What can I do to get through to you, Joan? I could not have stayed on with the Tories, not the way things have been going.'

'Heath did,' snapped Joan bitterly. 'So did Pym, Biffen and others. Why couldn't you?'

'They're coming to the end of their political lives. I'm still at the beginning. I couldn't live with myself, going on trying to defend Maggie all the time when I no longer agreed with her.'

'The constituency chairman's wife cut me dead this week. Crossed the road deliberately to avoid me when I saw her in the High Street.'

'Then she's not worth bothering about, is she?' said Will.

'I don't know how you can be so complacent,' snapped Joan. 'I don't blame her, frankly. You decide to switch to the SDP and still carry on as MP. I still don't know how you had the gall.'

'Very simple. As an MP I don't represent a party, I represent 90,000 constituents. Like Tony Benn said: 90,000 employers.'

'It all strikes me as a massive cheat. You're there under false pretences.'

'David Owen's wife didn't see it like that, or Bill Rodgers'.'

Joan looked out at the swirling sea.

'In any case it won't be long before it's all over,' said Will. 'She's bound to announce the date soon.'

'Don't count your chickens. Devon folk are very traditional. They've always gone for Liberals. When are they deciding?'

'Wednesday. The result'll be announced in the evening. And there's no chance I can lose this. They hardly know the Liberal down there. I'm a national figure. They're bound to go for me.'

'Oh, you think so,' laughed Joan. 'Pretty sure of yourself, aren't you? There've already been some nasty shocks in these parcelling-out arrangements of yours. Bloody pathetic. One seat for a Lib, one for the SDP; one for you, one for me.'

'Belittling bitch at times, aren't you?' Will snapped. 'Well, just wait. They wouldn't dream of turning me down. When it hasn't been a Liberal in Haverton, it's gone to a Tory. Strong Conservative tradition. That kind of background will have an appeal to the selectors.'

Joan laughed. 'Oh, I see. Now you're planning to get in behind the skirts of your Tory past. Well, I wouldn't choose you. Too bloody spineless.'

Will sat back. 'You've never had a good opinion of me, have you? Don't know why. I reckon I've always done my best by the constituents. Cared about them, taken time over them.'

'But never taken time over me. Scarcely seen you during the week. Not even able to make plans at the weekends. Could never have a meal ready at a particular time. Never knew two hours in advance where you'd be. Wouldn't have been here today if you hadn't been approached by the rambling club magazine.'

Will leaned across the table and touched her hand. She did not pull away. A tear formed and slowly coursed down her face. He spoke gently.

'You did know how it would be, all those years ago. I did warn you. We talked about it.'

'I know. And it seemed worth it while you were still in the Party. I thought they'd all become friends, all those Tories. They won't speak to either of us now.' Tears were flowing.

Will got up and edged into the seat closest to her.

'It's been a bad time. Sure it has. Not many of them talk to me in the House now either. Even the one or two Labour friends I had don't bother. John Henshaw has found an excuse each time lately when I've suggested a game of squash.'

Joan was upset at this. 'You used to play every week.'

'I know,' he said quietly. He was still holding her hand. 'Let's head towards a fresh start. Think of the Devon countryside. An election this year. Bound to be chosen as the candidate. It'll be a pushover.'

Through the tears Joan sounded bitter again. 'You assume such a lot, Will. Always have. The PM will call a June election, they'll select you in Haverton and not the Liberal, we'll be down there by the autumn.'

'That's right, love. That's just how I see it. I have every confidence.' His face was a broad smile.

Joan waited a moment. 'I won't be with you, Will.'

It took a moment before he felt stunned. He did not speak. His face asked the questions flooding in.

'I've had enough,' said the unhappy Joan. 'I didn't want to tell you today. I was going to leave it until the selection panel met this week. Then I was going to tell you.'

By now Will had released his hand from hers and was almost slumped back in his seat.

'Tell me what?' he asked, his gaping mouth finding difficulty forming the words.

'We both know it's over, Will. Come on now. What has there been in the last year or so?'

'Well, it's been a hard time, certainly. But all couples have hard times.' His words petered out.

'Hard times don't last this long, or shouldn't.'

'No, Joan, please. Give me a chance.'

'You've had your chance, Will.'

'Don't leave me.'

She spoke gently. 'Someone else wants me with him, Will.'

He stared at her. The question wasn't angry. 'Who?'

'Mike.'

His eyes became like sunray lamps. 'Mike Henderson? My agent?'

Joan nodded.

'How long?'

'About a year. A year next week. Friday.'

Will grasped around for the date, attempting to recall the same day the previous year. In the welter of confusion he gave up trying to reach back that far.

'You've been seeing Mike for a year?'

She looked down.

'Have you?'

'Yes, yes,' she said, momentarily alarmed. He so seldom raised his voice.

He was very quiet again. 'You must have covered your tracks very well.'

'Not really. All those long evening trips away. Friday after Friday. Leaving the House at four, then a journey to Birmingham, or wherever, for a speech, back home gone two in the morning.' She lowered her head. 'There was plenty of time.'

In a dazed state he asked her what she intended to do.

'Mike wants me to go and live with him. I was going to tell you next week and then move out.'

'Mike Henderson, eh? Opportunist little bugger.'

'Don't say that, please. He's like you in many ways: kind,

decent. He's got some of your weaknesses too. Never likes to cause a fuss.'

'That's a weakness?' Will said.

'Yes, frankly, when it's necessary to make a fuss.'

'Well, he's certainly caused one now,' he said with bitterness. 'So what's the difference, if we're both the same?'

'He was always there, Will. And you weren't.'

Will pleaded. The kick in the stomach had knocked pride out of the way. 'Please, Joan, think again. Don't go.'

'I can't help it, Will. I don't love you any more and I do love Mike.'

Will sat back helplessly. 'So what do we do now? The photographers at Crowlink?'

Joan smiled. 'Don't worry, I'll be there. A last public duty if you like. But it won't do us any good spending the next two hours together. We need to think and talk later.'

'Will there be anything left to talk about?' he asked unhappily.

'Well, let's see how it goes. I'm pushing off now to do the walk. We'll both need to be alone. If you can't face walking now, you know how to get there. Bus to Friston Pond then down the path by the church.' She got up.

'So that's it for the present? Just like that? I meet you at Crowlink at two o'clock. All smiles in front of the cameras?' There was sarcasm in his voice.

'Like you've always said, Will; politics and show business. All a question of keeping up appearances.'

'So what happens after the magazine have got their pictures?' he asked.

'Let's take that as it comes. I'll see you up there, Will.'

With that she was away out of the door, walking boots clumping. A lump the size of an apple swelled his throat at the sight of the boots. That was how they had met. A fell-walking weekend with the Young Conservatives. He looked away at the sea, trying to force the memory from his mind. Unhappiness welled along with the tears. He took out a handkerchief and tried to hide what was happening. Sitting back in the chair he rehearsed, over and over, the scene that had just finished. Then he action-replayed the last ten years. It was impossible. He could not do it all in one chunk. Twenty minutes passed, half an hour. The place was filling up with lunch customers. He found himself becoming increasingly exhausted with unhappiness and memories. He was at his lowest ebb when a waitress bent down towards him.

'Excuse me, are you Mr Forbes?'

'Yes,' he said, startled.

'There's a telephone call for you. The manageress says you can come through to the kitchen to take it.'

'Thank you,' said Will and followed her to the kitchen. Then he froze. There was only one person with whom he had left the telephone numbers of all possible contact points on this Sunday. He had told Mike Henderson to ring if there were any developments over the selection. His wife had just told him she was about to leave him for this man, and now he was phoning him. Will started to feel sick. On reaching the kitchen he picked up the receiver with both hands; he was trembling and feared dropping the instrument. He made every attempt to speak matter-of-factly.

'Will Forbes here.'

'Will, it's Mike,' came the expected reply.

'Hullo, Mike.' No 'how-are-you?' this time.

Henderson spotted the awkwardness. 'Are you OK?' he asked.

'Yes, fine. What are you ringing about?'

'Bad news, I'm afraid. I've been getting whispers from the constituency.' There was a pause. 'They don't want you, Will.'

'What are you talking about, don't want me.'

'It's that simple, old lad.'

'Don't patronise me, tell me what it's about,' he shouted, causing the kitchen staff to look round.

At the other end of the line Mike Henderson was confused. He had called Will 'old lad' for years.

'Er, well, sorry. The fact is that the party workers in Haverton have been making investigations about you. They've gone back over the years to find out what your record is like.'

'What record? What have they been looking into?'

'Everything,' said Henderson awkwardly. 'You see, they're generally suspicious of anyone who changes tack halfway through anything. That set them off finding out about everything you've ever joined.'

Will was beginning to understand. 'Go on.'

'Well, they found out about the Leisure and Work Society, the League Against Cruel Sports, Amnesty and a string of others. They've discovered you didn't stay with any of them for more than a year or two.'

Will was silent.

'And so, the word is that you're not consistent. And, well, they couldn't trust you.'

Will took so long to reply that Henderson asked him if he had heard. Will nodded, realised that was not effective, and quietly said yes. Then pulling himself together:

'So all the Parliamentary work, the two Private Members' Bills I worked my guts out to push through, all that means nothing?'

'It looks that way, except that we're really going to have to work on that for Wednesday's meeting. We shall have to hammer at that.'

Wednesday: It seemed like an age away. Will wanted to chuck it in now, but Henderson was the person who would receive the satisfaction. Instead he agreed.

'I'll meet you off the train at Victoria tonight,' said Henderson. 'What time are you getting back?'

'No,' said Will quickly, 'leave it tonight, I'll see you in the morning.'

'But we ought to start on our strategy tonight,' protested Henderson.

'Leave it, Mike, leave it till the morning,' said Will firmly. He wanted to scream it at him but controlled himself.

'All right,' replied Henderson, baffled at Will's behaviour. 'See you tomorrow then.'

Will replaced the receiver. He reflected how at the end of such calls Henderson always asked Will to give Joan his love. He did not say it this time.

He thanked the kitchen staff who were all looking at him, together with various others who had arrived to gaze at the celebrity in their midst. They saw his face, but not the pain that was searing up behind it. He walked back into the restaurant and dazedly out into the open, attempting to find a secluded park bench on the western lawns.

The feeling of devastation kept coming at him like a speeding train, like two in fact, one from each direction. He could not comprehend it all. This morning he had a wife and the prospect of a new safe seat in Devon. Now, nothing.

He sat for some time before dragging himself up in desperation. The feeling of stupor would not leave him. In his dazed state he walked across the road into Wilmington Square. On one level he was not aware of anything. On another he observed every detail: the cracks in the pavement, the thin peeling line of paint on the pillar box. His strides were measured and slow. All the years of marriage about to be lost; the same with his political life. He found himself in front of the Congress Theatre and gazed at the display boards. There was going to be a big show that night, a Royal Command thing with Princess Margaret attending. There was a certain amount of coming and going. He looked around and thought he saw a famous face. A film star was it, or somebody in sport? He could not be sure and did not care. Perhaps someone involved in the show. He gave the celebrity, whoever he was, no more thought.

Instead he ambled along Carlisle Road which he remembered eventually led another way to Beachy Head. In his low state he had forgotten about Joan's suggestion to get the bus. Instead he walked, thinking and thinking, wondering what future there was for him.

L. J.

'What made you invite her round?' asked John irritably. 'She's such a pain in the neck.'

'Don't exaggerate,' replied his wife. 'She's not that bad. She's lonely.'

'I'm not surprised, Jill. She's so opinionated. Who's going to cope with her except mugs like us?'

Jill took the casserole out of the oven and checked it. 'She's my friend and has been good to me. She's stimulating and has plenty to say that's interesting.'

'Correction: she has plenty to say.'

Somewhat exasperated, Jill did not reply. She put the casserole back.

'Are you coming back in?' said John. 'I can't take it much more on my own. They're already showing signs of getting at each other's throats.'

'O.K. I'll be in in a minute. Just want to do the salad.'

John took the bottle of sherry rescued from the cupboard and went back into the lounge. There was an uncomfortable silence.

'More sherry, Keeley?'

'No thanks,' replied his guest.

'Ready for a fill-up, L. J?' He turned to the only other person in the room.

'Yes please, John,' said the man.

The host poured out two glasses, gave one to L. J., and sat down with the other glass in his hand.

'Lunch won't be long,' he ventured, after a gap.

'Fine,' said L. J. Keeley looked out of the window.

'Jill's just putting the finishing touches,' John laughed. 'She'll be back in a minute.' Another pause.

'So how did you get on this week, L. J?' Should be firm enough ground, thought John. Get him to talk about his work. Plenty of scope there.

L. J. came to life. 'Oh, all right,' he mused. 'God-awful Agatha Christie thriller. But it packed the place out most nights.'

'Good,' said John. 'It's a smashing theatre, isn't it?'

'One of the best, the Devonshire Park, and I mean *the* best,' expanded L. J. taking off his dark glasses for a moment and replacing them after rubbing his nose. 'All you Eastbournians want to look after that place. It's a goody.'

'What are you going to do next?' asked Keeley half-heartedly.

'That's just it, nothing,' replied L. J. 'Absolutely nothing on the books at all.'

'So what will you do?' Keeley persisted.

'The dole, as from tomorrow.'

Jill came into the room and picked up the conversation as well as a glass. 'You're unemployed now, L. J?' she queried.

'Absolutely,' he said. 'Don't know what I'm going to do for money.'

'You must have made a packet after five years in the soap thing,' snorted Keeley.

'Don't you believe it.' L. J. almost spat out the words. 'It's not that good. And I spent a fortune all that time travelling up to Birmingham.'

John came in on L. J's side. 'Yes, I s'pose we easily get the idea it's all glamour and big money.'

'It's a bloody sight better paid and more glamorous than the poor Asian women in sweat shops in the East End.' This from Keeley, eyes blazing.

'O-o-o-h. She *has* got a moody on, hasn't she?' said L. J., camping it up as the mood had taken him.

'Well, it's true, isn't it?' said Keeley. 'All you entertainment people seem to think you're hard done by.'

'Oh!' exclaimed L.J. 'And how many do you know?'

'Well,' said Keeley, a touch defensively, 'one or two I've seen in the pub in Camden. They're all so pretentious.'

'Huh!' exploded L.J. 'What's pretentious about me?'

'Since you ask, why do you call yourself L.J? It's got such a tiresome American ring about it. Why couldn't you call yourself Leonard or Lionel, or whatever your name is?'

'Because it's different, and because I choose not to,' rapped L.J.

Keeley looked away.'

'Hey, come on,' said John. 'This is supposed to be a pleasant Sunday lunch party. Let's talk about something else. Anyone see anything good on television this week?'

Keeley yawned.

'What about the Oscars?' said Jill, pushing the boat out brav-ely. 'Wasn't it awful?'

L.J. rose to the occasion again. 'My God, yes. I caught most of it after getting back to my digs. Thought the production side of it this time was hideous.'

'And the sound was so distorted,' continued Jill. 'There seemed to be lots of other things happening in the background.'

'Pity about our own guy losing to de Niro,' said John.

'Henley Beaufort?' said L.J. 'Yes, he made no attempt to hide his disappointment, did he? I did a season in rep with him years ago, long before he made the big time. I seem to recall he said he was from around this area.'

'What was he like?' asked Jill.

'Oh, all right, in those days, I s'pose. Tended to drift off when you were talking to him. Bit neurotic.'

Keeley snorted. 'But you're all neurotic, aren't you?'

'Is that another of your lunchtime pleasantries?' asked L.J.

'No, seriously. I'm not getting at you especially,' Keeley defended herself. 'But it's a fact, isn't it, about actors. You couldn't do it otherwise, surely.'

'I expect there are a lot of actors who aren't neurotic, Keeley,' laughed Jill.

'But there must be something,' Keeley continued, warming to her theme. 'An affectation common to you all. Why do *you* have to wear dark glasses, for instance, now, indoors?'

'Why do I call myself L.J? Why do I wear dark glasses? Why do I have to justify myself to you?'

'Sorry,' said Keeley, getting up. 'Just making conversation. Excuse me a minute.' She made for the kitchen. Jill followed her saying she ought to check something.

'Jesus!' declared L.J. 'Where did you dig her up?'

'Sorry, L.J.' apologised John. 'I find her very hard work too. She's Jill's friend. They met up at a feminist group.'

'Oh, God,' said L.J. 'Jill's not one of those fanatics, is she?'

'Not now. She left it a couple of months ago. Said it was all getting heavy. Bordering on lesbianism.'

L.J. laughed. 'Well, I'm not surprised. Bunch of freaks!'

'Hey, hey, come on. Wouldn't do you any harm to be more tolerant.'

'You don't believe in all that stuff, do you?' asked L.J.

'Not all the intensity that goes with it, no, but deep down I do. Worked in an office in London when I first left school. There was a woman who was number two in the department. The manager left and everyone thought she'd get the job. Red hot she was at her work. They passed her over, just 'cause she was a woman. I'll never forget her face when she came back from the personnel manager's office. It was so unjust. A week later she handed in her notice. She'd been there eighteen years.' John finished his sherry. 'Fancy another?'

'Yes, sure,' said L.J. 'You're right, of course. I shouldn't be scathing. My own business is as bad. Wardrobe is always run by a woman, the carpenter is always a bloke. But why do they have to be so bloody intense about it?'

'Frustration, I s'pose,' said John. 'Some of them reckon they've been aware of it two hundred years or more, yet they didn't really move their backsides on it until the late sixties. That's a long time to build up pressure.'

'Is that why you keep up with this Keeley?'

'Oh, I don't. Can't stand the woman. Jill likes her. Or rather, feels sorry for her.'

L.J. laughed quietly.

'What about you, L.J? What are you going to do?'

His friend sighed. He took his glasses off. This time they stayed off. 'Things are looking grim now.'

'No more Agatha Christie then?'

'No. We finished with the old lady last night. That's why I don't have to travel to bloody Chesterfield, or Newcastle.'

'Oh, sorry, you did tell me. That's why you're able to make it today?'

'Yeah.'

'No spin-offs from the play on the telly this week?'

'Not a carrot.'

'Pity. We both liked what you did in it. We really did. Enjoyed your performance.'

L.J. smiled. 'Thanks, mate. Sweet of you.' He was becoming abstracted. 'I don't know if I did the right thing in leaving *Beachlands*.'

'Five years must be a long time on one programme,' said John. 'You were aching to get out of it a long while.'

45

'Yes, I know. But it was such regular money. Not colossal, as I was trying to point out to Your Friend earlier.'

'Jill's friend,' interjected John. They laughed.

'Jill's friend then. But I knew it was coming in every week. And the effect of Freddie's death was enormous at the time.'

'God, wasn't it?' echoed John. 'Headlines in all the papers. The programme kept making reference to you, er, Freddie, for ages afterwards.'

'I lived off the fame, even if not the money, for nearly a year after that. But even that has died as well.'

He began to sound wistful. 'I don't think anyone recognised me this week in the play. At one time if I was doing theatre, they used to applaud when I first came on. The youngsters even screamed and cheered. You could have heard a pin drop when I came on this week.'

John stayed silent, not knowing what to say.

L.J. saved him from an embarrassing silence. 'I really do think about chucking it all in sometimes.'

'Well, perhaps that wouldn't be such a bad idea,' John ventured. 'Have a complete break, try something entirely different. You could go into computers. They're still crying out for people. All kinds of training schemes are starting up.'

L.J. shook his head wearily. 'No, that's not for me. Showing myself off in public is all I'm interested in.'

'Sounds a bit obscene,' observed John with a laugh. 'But if you chuck it in, you'd have to do something else.'

'I didn't mean it like that, John – chucking it in. I meant life; ending it all.'

John shifted uneasily. This was not L.J. being flippant. 'Oh, come on, fella. You don't want to talk like that, surely.'

'No, I don't. I'd much rather be in a different frame of mind altogether. I'd much rather be in completely different circumstances so I didn't feel this way. But I *am* feeling this way and I *am* in these circumstances.'

'Well, what about theatre management?' said John. 'If there's no work for you, why not try that? And you'd still be working closely in the field you like most.'

'Standing in a foyer in a monkey suit every night?' L.J. shook his head. 'No, I wouldn't fancy that.'

46

John tried a different tack. 'There's never been anyone in your life? Nobody you've felt close to?'

'No,' said L.J. 'No woman has come my way whom I've felt I wanted to spend the rest of my life with. Haven't even had an affair in over a year.'

John looked awkwardly at L.J., then bit his lip.

L.J. picked it up and laughed. 'No, I'm not gay either. I can see you wondering.'

John coloured a little and smiled tentatively. 'Sorry.'

'It's all right, John,' reassured L.J. 'Everyone wonders it about me. Thirty-five, never married, flamboyant. But no, I don't experience strong feelings for woman *or* men.'

'A pity that,' said John. 'You might feel differently if there was someone you cared about and who cared about you.'

'Sure,' came the reply. 'But it isn't like that, and I can't force it.' He gave a deep sigh. 'I feel so empty. It doesn't bother me not to have a relationship with someone. It's always been in me to be alone, just to go back to the flat, look at the four walls and remember who I am again. I value it. But until a few months ago I always had something to think about: a new project of one sort or another. Now it's all dried up, and so have I. Do you remember Ronnie Brogan?'

John shook his head.

'No, not many do now. He was quite big in the fifties and early sixties. Plenty of TV revues and feature parts in Rank films. He once said that in one year there were only two days he didn't have to drive to Pinewood. Now I see him mooching about in Ladbroke Grove as I go home. Always catch him on a Friday afternoon and always under that grotty bridge by the tube. God! He looks a sight in his old raincoat. I try to avoid him sometimes. It's embarrassing.'

He looked directly into his friend's eyes. 'I'm not going to end up like that, John. Not in sheer emptiness. And I can see it happening.'

'But L.J.,' protested John, 'it's so futile to be defeatist. We saw someone who talked like that on the box this week. You couldn't have seen it, you were working. An interview with Greg Horsham.'

L.J. rubbed the bridge of his nose. 'Oh, yeah. He was in the England team until a couple of years ago.'

'That's him,' continued John. 'Well, I was amazed at the change in him. He had a great future once. Then he had this terrible accident doing a stunt for the BBC. On Wednesday he looked dreadful. Would never have recognised him.'

'Yes, I do recall him now,' said L.J. 'Good-looking bugger with long blond hair.'

'Right, only now he's let himself go. The looks are still there, he's about our age, but all the hope seems to have gone out of him.'

'That's right,' said L.J. quietly.

'But it's no good, L.J., that sort of attitude. The interviewer suggested he took up TV commentating. He pointed out how good he was at communicating. The team always liked him as a captain. But the bloke just shrugged his shoulders.'

'I know the feeling,' said L.J.

'But it's so negative. You can't afford to drift on like that.'

'It's all very well for you. You're not shipwrecked.'

'Oh, come on, mate. What can I do to pull you out of this? I've known you so many years. I can't see you like this.'

L.J. was about to speak when the women reappeared in earnest debate. L.J. put his glasses back on.

'No thanks, Jill, you can keep your bloody Will Forbes with his half-baked ideas.' Keeley was in full blood. Jill raised her eyes at John as she came into the room.

'The only way we're going to get anywhere is by consensus,' protested Jill wearily.

'Have you been hard at it?' laughed John.

'We were talking about Will Forbes' performance on *Question Time* this week,' explained Jill. 'I said how impressed we both were with him.'

'Huh, just because you helped him on the campaign trail years ago,' said Keeley.

'That has nothing to do with it,' answered John sharply. 'Yes, I did help him when we were at the City Poly together. That was years ago. I happen to admire what he stands for. His sort is the only real answer to Thatcherism.'

'God help us then,' exclaimed Keeley.

'Right,' broke in Jill, 'I think it's about time we sat down. L.J., would you like to come to the table and sit there?'

Jill indicated the place as L.J. got slowly to his feet.

'And what were you both talking about before we came in?'
She smiled as she tried hard to recreate an agreeable atmosphere.

L.J. found it difficult to answer. John chipped in. 'Oh, we were talking about TV as well, the sports stars programme.'

L.J. was just sitting down. Jill motioned Keeley to sit opposite him.

'Yes, it was good, wasn't it? And did you tell him about the remarkable interview with Greg Horsham?' she said, almost absently.

'Oh, yes,' mumbled John awkwardly. 'I did mention it.'

'What was remarkable about it?' asked Keeley.

'He was in such a state,' Jill plunged on. 'He had all the appearance of someone about to commit suicide.'

John looked hard at the soup bowl in front of him.

'Did he say so?' asked Keeley.

'Not in those words. But he was so acutely depressed, wasn't he, John?'

'Yes, yes,' said John. 'Do you want the pepper, L.J?'

His friend shook his head.

'He just had the look of someone who'd given up all hope,' said Jill, unaware of the minefield she was ploughing through.

'I've got no time for people like that,' offered Keeley. 'With so much going on that's really awful, our problems are very small beans.'

'Oh, you can't say that,' said Jill, as John wished hard he was somewhere else. He snatched a quick look over to L.J. who was very quiet and toying with his soup.

'After all,' Jill continued, 'when we're in despair, how can we drag ourselves out of it by thinking of Ethiopia?'

'If we concentrated on Ethiopia to start with,' proclaimed Keeley, 'we wouldn't get into the state of giving up hope for our own puny lives.'

John felt rage welling up and beginning to take over his awkwardness. 'You do talk rubbish at times.' He glared at her. 'When was the last time you had to put yourself to the test?'

'I would never let myself get to that stage,' Keeley flared. 'And I'll tell you this. Anyone who commits suicide is bloody selfish.'

'Jesus!' cried John. 'How can you make such a sweeping

statement? What do you know of the state of mind of someone who has reached a low point?'

'I've no time for that,' scoffed Keeley. 'There are too many agencies around, and too many people you can talk to today. There aren't the inhibitions of years ago. People can discuss their problems quite easily if they have to. No, it's sheer bloody selfishness if you kill yourself nowadays.'

John was at a loss, embarrassed and drained by the thought of his sad friend next to him. Jill was annoyed into silence. In the sudden quiet L.J. got to his feet.

'I'm sorry, Jill. You'll have to excuse me. I don't feel too good. I can't manage the rest of the meal.' He was out of the door before Jill could protest. But John was there, racing after him. He caught up with him just before he reached the gate.

'Come on, fella. You don't want to take any notice. She's an insensitive bitch, that's all.'

'I can't take the atmosphere,' said the unhappy L.J. 'I need to take a long long walk and get some air, perhaps along the seafront.'

'Well, all right,' John caved in. 'But please give me a ring before you go back to London tonight.'

'Maybe,' said L.J., now seeming quite detached.

'Not maybe,' insisted John. 'Do it. Give me a call.'

'Maybe,' L.J. said again as he turned and walked dejectedly along the road. John stayed at the gate until he was out of sight. L.J. did not look back as he walked slowly towards Carlisle Road.

GREG

The train pulled into Eastbourne station. He was among the last to get off. He avoided crowds now if he could. All that staring from everybody. No, perhaps it was not the staring so much as the looks of puzzlement as they strained to recall where they had seen him before. He sighed. Why should he worry about that now? There was only this emptiness left.

He came out of the station. Nobody was staring. They had more important things on their minds, especially the older folk, preoccupied with their suitcases and need for transport to take them to their hotels. He noticed that there were a lot of elderly people, probably here for one of the cheaper weeks before the season got started. A faint temporary smile glowed inside him. Greg always had felt warmth for the older folk. They were the ones he could relate to in the pub on training days. At lunch-times one would buttonhole him and show genuine enthusiasm for the game, talk about United's former glories, face alight with life. Much better than all the cynics of the younger generation. It was a momentary thought as he recalled again why he was here. The party of four older people in front of him got into their taxi and he was now at the head of the queue.

As the next taxi drew up he got into the front passenger seat. He soon wished he had not.

'Bloody glad I've got you and not those old buggers in front. Yellow perils we call them, that Saga lot. Don't get no tips out of them.'

Time was when Greg would have argued. He was beyond the effort now.

The driver looked at him expecting a response but immediately forgot about it. Instead he delivered a double-take.

'Blimey! You're Greg Horsham, aren't you?'

'That's right.'

'Don't often get football celebrities in the cab. Plenty of well-known poofy actors for the summer seasons.'

Greg wondered if there was anybody this bigot did like. Probably footballers were about the nearest.

'Nothing much of a celebrity these days,' Greg smiled, as the driver let the brake off and pulled out of the station forecourt.

'Yeah, you 'ad a run of bad luck coupla seasons ago.'

'You could say that.'

'Where d'ya wanna go, by the way?'

'Can you just drive around for a bit?' answered Greg.

The driver was pleased. Nowhere in particular meant the meter clocking up indefinitely, and since his own main interest was football, he would be able to pump his celebrity passenger about it.

'Sure, whatever you like. Fancy a spin round the country a bit?'

'Yes, fine.'

The driver headed in the direction of Friston. 'So what's been happening to you lately?' he enquired.

'I had an interview on TV this week,' Greg answered.

'Go on! When was that then?'

Greg half laughed. 'It was one of those "Whatever happened to . . ." programmes about people who used to be well known.'

'Get away. You're still well known. Why did they stick you in something like that?'

'Nobody knows a fourth-rate footballer these days. Not unless they're followers of the game.' He turned his head to the driver. 'Like you presumably?'

'Oh, yeah. I look at what's going on generally. Get over to see Brighton play whenever I can.'

'Anyway, the TV people approached me about this ex-sports stars slot and I recorded it about ten days ago.'

'Sorry I missed that,' said the driver. 'What night was it on?'

'Wednesday, 8.30.'

'I was still workin' then.'

Greg looked out of the window as the taxi moved towards the Downs, and he thought of the times when he too was always working. How he had loved his life then. Hard work it was, but so invigorating. All his energies went into training and the games. Well, not quite all. Some of it was left over for . . . He smiled at the thought. It was an exhilarating five-year period over his late twenties and early thirties. So many people, and then getting picked for England and going all over the world. He would never have travelled like that otherwise and seen all those places. Suddenly it had all come to an abrupt end two years ago. He could have coped with that if only . . .

'Will you ever lose the limp?'

Greg started, as though woken up. He had heard what the driver said but pretended not to.

'Sorry, what was that?'

'The limp in your leg? Will they be able to straighten it out completely?'

'Oh, that,' said Greg. 'They've managed that already. You probably didn't notice. The doctors have told me to keep walking. I do plenty of that anyway and it does do it good. Not that it matters now.'

The driver shot him a sideways glance as Greg drifted into thought again.

Pat had not wanted him to do the stunt and had said so from the start. There had been pleadings every night for a week; but Greg had been adamant.

'Look,' he had said one night, 'I want to experience all I can in sports activity. I've told you this before. I know I can't cover it all, but I've got this chance to do a parachute jump and I'm going to go for it. I want to do it.'

Pat had remained unmoved.

He saw himself again getting nearer the ground. The instructor had told him not to jerk the ropes too quickly, but he could see concrete and grass rushing towards him. He wanted to make sure of the grass. He panicked and tugged hard. The instructor could not help now, nor the BBC, filming the event for their stunts show. Greg looked out of the car window and could see the sea beyond the Downs. Once again he winced as he heard the exploding crack of his body on the concrete.

He should have listened to Pat. Now he had lost even the one person who had meant more than anyone in his life.

The driver tried again. 'You were in plaster a long time.'

'Covered in it, my left leg was. Toe to waist. They reckoned it was a miracle the leg could be saved. In hospital for months. Then on crutches for nearly a year after that. Put paid to the football.'

'Won't you ever play again?' asked the driver.

'By the time I could, nobody would want me. Thirty-five now and out of training so long.'

'Must have been a bloody awful long time for you,' observed the driver, a touch of sensitivity showing through. He genuinely felt sorry for the man. 'Did you get any support from the other players?'

'Yes, a lot. They were a great bunch of lads, and their wives and girlfriends. They all rallied round.' Greg paused briefly. 'Then there was Pat.'

'Is that your wife?'

Greg almost jumped at the irony. 'No, no, I'm not married.'

The driver half laughed. The familiarity with a famous person was not too different from that towards a personal friend. 'Got an understanding with 'er, 'ave you?' he said with a wink.

Well, you asked for it, thought Greg. 'You know Pat Sheridan, United's goalkeeper?'

Realisation spread slowly over the driver's face. 'What, ya mean you . . . live with 'im?'

'I did,' replied Greg, the pain entering him again. 'Not any more.'

The taxi turned off the main road at the village of East Dean, into the country lane leading to Birling Gap. Greg looked out of the window again, not giving a damn about the driver's stunned silence.

Pat Sheridan! What a guy! Greg remembered how he had warmed to him the first time he came into the room at the club. The manager introduced him to them all. Greg recalled it as though it was yesterday: the firm handshake, the blue eyes staring into his own and the crop of red hair. Pat had smiled at him warmly. They got on well together from the first.

And what a great bunch his team mates had been. They could see what was happening. They knew how it was when Greg and Pat always insisted on a hotel room together for away matches. They even grew protective towards them when the whispers started. Often a tabloid reporter had finished up on the pavement while nosing around too much and firing too many questions. Good guys.

Pat had not taken long to show he felt the same way. Greg invited him round one evening and as the drink flowed Pat spoke of his failed marriage and his failure to consummate it. The doctor had said: 'Don't worry. It'll be OK once you're married.' Pat had been twenty at the time.

This feeling for Pat had been unique for Greg. He had been through the clubs, several one-night stands and the masseurs.

He had stopped all that a good three years before the Big A got going, thanks to Pat's arrival. And when Pat came along, he was not self-conscious any longer. There was no more self-justification.

Greg was aware that the taxi had stopped.

'This is Birling Gap,' the driver said, trying to sound as indifferent as possible.

Greg looked at the three or four old houses perched on the edge of the cliff and as he started to speak he realised he had no interest in their history as he might once have done. He held back.

'What's that?' asked the driver.

'Nothing.' replied Greg. He sighed and rubbed his eyes.

'What d'you wanna do now?'

Greg shrugged. He thought it was about time to get on with it. 'Are we anywhere near Beachy Head?' he asked.

'Yeah, it's up this road, the coast road. Winds a bit over the cliffs. Only about five minutes.'

'All right,' said Greg.

The driver turned away from the stony car park and started towards Beachy Head. He was struggling with his thoughts. He knew what queers were like: limp wristed and fancy scarves round their necks. He had seen enough of them when he drove a cab in the West End. Mincing walks and lispy voices. But this bloke was not like that. He looked like a man. And he was a footballer. He had seen Greg Horsham on telly often. He was strong, with thighs like tree trunks.

'How can *you* be a poofter?' The question was blurted out before he even thought about it.

There was faint irony in Greg's voice. 'It's easy, my friend, if you're made that way.'

'But, Jesus, I've seen you playing football. Not just on the telly. I saw you a couple of times when you played against Brighton. You're well built. You took a lot of aggro and bruising and that. You didn't make a sound.'

'So?' Greg decided to let the fellow bluster along.

'Well, bloody hell, you *act* like a man, not a raving fairy.'

Greg paused. 'You'd be surprised how many don't behave like fairies. Some are fortunate to be physically fit like me and have a lot of stamina. Some are at the other end of the scale:

effeminate, camp. Most are in the middle: ordinary, unnotice-able, like anyone. You run into them every day, but you don't know it.'

'Bloody do an' all. I can pick 'em out straightaway.'

'Really? *I* surprised you, didn't I?'

The driver's confusion was increasing. After a while he spoke again.

'You say you split up from Pat Sheridan?'

'A month or two ago.' The pain was back the moment he said it. Greg did not intend to go into it with this moron, so he said no more. The driver was bursting with confusion and curiosity.

'How can you do it? How can you do what we do . . . with women?'

'I don't expect straight guys to understand,' said Greg. 'If you've never felt it for another bloke, there's no reason for you even to imagine what it's like.'

The driver stayed silent as the taxi climbed up past the dis-used lighthouse.

'But I tell you this,' Greg decided to continue, 'the love I still feel for Pat is so warm and good and true that *you* could never make me think it's anything other than natural, for me. I don't ask any other blokes to feel the same way.'

'You still . . . love 'im then,' The driver grimaced as he said it.

Greg looked out of the window. His 'yes' was scarcely aud-ible. The driver frowned. 'So you're having a bad time, like, er, a husband and wife breaking up.' He gulped and cleared his throat.

Greg looked at the driver who saw the reply in Greg's eyes. The driver was more confused. He was not just disgusted. He found himself feeling sorry for the footballer. He pulled into the bus stop area at the top of the cliffs. The place was empty, the summer buses not yet brought out.

'This is it, Beachy Head. I take it you want to have a look.'

Greg nodded.

'Well, I'll stay here while you go across.'

'It's OK,' sighed Greg. 'I'll pay you now.' He mumbled some-thing about finding his own way back and paid the driver.

'Suit yourself,' said the driver.

Greg got out of the car, climbed the small embankment and walked slowly over to the cliff top.

The driver was about to pull away, but was so dazed by the whole episode that he switched the engine off and got out of the car as well. He went up on to the embankment and stood looking as Greg came back into view. This was something new for him. Up to now he had felt only contempt for Greg's kind. He could not work out why he was feeling sorry for him. He took out a cigarette and lit up. He followed Greg's slow progress across to the cliffs. He watched him reach the edge, look over, pace up and down a few times. What was he doing now? Coming back apparently, facing the sea and doing a sort of jog towards the edge again. The taxi driver's mouth opened in all four directions, releasing the cigarette which fell to the ground in front of him. With hands shaking he ran like fury to reach Greg.

'No,' he screamed as he raced towards him. But Greg had already stopped at the edge as the driver caught up with him still shouting 'No.' It seemed the only thing to shout.

'Don't do that!' he gasped. 'That's hopeless.' The driver's blood was racing.

Greg looked at him. 'I thought you'd gone.' His own voice was shaking. 'I thought you'd driven off. I . . . I didn't think anyone was looking.'

A few people were looking now as the driver got hold of Greg's arm. 'Please,' he said, 'come back to the car.'

Greg had enough of his faculties left to realise he did not have a chance of killing himself while he had an audience and allowed himself to be led back to the car. Once at the foot of the embankment they were out of the gaze of the sightseers. The driver opened the door of the passenger side allowing Greg to get in. Then he quickly moved to his own door and settled back in his seat. He could not recall the last time he had had to be so alert. But now he did not know how to go on. How could he stop someone killing himself if he was determined? And why should he?

'Don't think of doing it,' he pleaded.

'There's nothing else left,' said the unhappy Greg. 'I don't want to live any more.'

'But you must do. Everyone wants to live.'

Greg looked at the driver, his face contorted with pain.

'I mean, well, what can I say, it's just not natural to kill yourself.'

'*You* don't think it's natural to love the way I do.'

'Yeah, I know,' he blustered, 'but once you're dead, there's nothing . . . it's, oh, I dunno. Isn't there anyone in your life now?'

Greg shook his head.

'But someone might come along, just like your mate, er, your friend.'

'I don't want anyone after Pat. There's no one like him. My life's nothing now.'

'But I've heard women say that about blokes and vice versa. Blimey, my own daughter said it a month ago when she broke up with her boyfriend.'

Greg did not answer.

'Look, let's drive back into town and just . . . talk for a while, shall we?'

Greg shrugged his shoulders. The driver switched on the engine and pulled away. 'There's no point in it,' he said again. 'It's awful.'

'It's awful living,' answered Greg. 'I've got nothing now.'

'You've got your life, that's what you've got,' said the driver. 'How old did you say you are, thirty-five?'

Greg nodded.

'Well, you could meet anybody, somebody for years yet.'

'Or I could meet nobody and end up an old man, lonely.'

'Yeah, well we all could. *I* will if my wife dies first.'

'It's not the same.'

'No, all right. I can see that.'

After a pause Greg said: 'In any case, I've got more problems. A shoplifting charge. I'm up before the bench tomorrow.'

'Oh, bloody 'ell,' said the driver. 'How did you get involved in something like that?'

'I don't know. I really don't. I was in this store. Three weeks ago it was. My head was swimming. Suddenly I was at the front door, walking off with these goods. Shop detective spotted me. That was it. Case comes up tomorrow.'

'Well, surely you can say you were ill, depressed, something like that.'

'I thought of doing that,' said Greg. 'But they could still find me guilty. I couldn't take that.'

'Even so, killing yerself, it can't be worth that. Nothing can be.' The driver felt himself losing ground fast.

Greg started to cry. He sobbed uncontrollably. 'I can't . . . Nothing's going right.'

'Here, come on.' The driver was out of his depth. A grown man crying. He had never seen such a thing before. All these new experiences were crowding in on him. Another taxi overtook and its driver waved and saw the crying figure. Greg's driver waved back and looked embarrassed.

'I'm sorry,' Greg whimpered, calming down.

'That's all right,' said the driver. There was another silence. The car was beginning its descent through the winding Duke's Drive with its tall trees stretching high for sunlight. Soon they would be at the top of Holywell cliffs where the seafront started.

'Try not to get too worked up over this shoplifting thing. Tell them how it is just now. They'll be able to see for themselves what you're like.'

Greg was beginning to feel dazed. If the driver had not been there on the cliff, it would have been all over by now. But the crying had calmed him down a bit. And with the calm had come more confusion.

The taxi headed downhill as the road descended in line with the cliffs until it reached sea level at the Wish Tower.

'Look,' said Greg. 'Don't take me back to the station. I'll get out over there, by that theatre.'

The driver had just turned into Wilmington Square. Uneasiness swept over him.

'I don't like this. I don't like leaving you.'

Greg mumbled: 'It'll be all right.'

The driver brought the vehicle to a stop. He took out a piece of card and a pencil.

'Look here, this is my name and phone number. Do me a favour and phone me tomorrow after the case is over. I want to know how you get on.'

Greg took the paper, made a poor attempt at a smile and started to find some money from his pockets.

'No, that's all right,' said the driver. 'It's on the house. Just so long as you phone me tomorrow. I'll be in around five. Please don't forget.'

Greg nodded. He found the handle and wearily got out of the car. The driver got out, stood by his door and shouted.

'Phone me. Please.'

Greg did not look back but raised his hand.

The driver watched him for a moment, got back in and drove off, uneasy and confused.

Greg moved around the groups gathered outside the Congress Theatre, then, still deep in unhappy thought, headed along Carlisle Road.

SOMEONE

He was glad to get away from the Congress Theatre. All those people milling around waiting for Princess Margaret. She wouldn't be there for hours yet. They were all eager for famous-face spotting. Royal occasions lent themselves to it. He had managed to get away before too many of them recognised him.

By contrast Carlisle Road was peaceful. The wind was giving way to a warm afternoon, and the spring blossom on the trees lining the avenues of the Meads area was outstanding. He began to feel a curious sense of peace settling on him. He knew what he was going to do. Another hour or so and all this pain would be over, all the frustrations of life. It was almost something to look forward to. He might even enjoy the walk, this last walk, on such a lovely afternoon.

Fifteen minutes after he passed the intersection, two young men emerged from Grassington Road. The warm weather had allowed them to be in shirtsleeve order but their helmets still made them feel hot. One of them was feeling awkward and found conversation difficult.

'Not many people about,' he offered.

His companion did not answer.

After a couple of minutes of progress along Carlisle Road he tried again. 'Tree blossom looks good.'

Still nothing. He could not take it any more. 'Oh, come on, Phil. You haven't said a word since we left the station. If we're having to work together we can't go on like this.'

'Why should I have anything to say to you?'

'Look, mate,' his colleague protested. 'I know it must have been bad for you but . . .'

'What the hell would you know about it?' Phil stopped in his tracks. 'Has anyone ever done the same to you?'

'No,' said the other. 'But I can imagine it.'

'Huh,' growled Phil and walked on again, leaving his companion to catch up. When the latter did so, he caught Phil's arm but Phil pulled abruptly away.

'Look, Roy. Mandy decided. She didn't want to go out with

me any more because she wants to go out with you. Let's leave it at that. All right?'

'No, of course it's not all right. You're feeling rough about it and I'm sorry. But it must be better that it has finished now, before you decided to get engaged or anything.'

'We were fine until you came along. Nearly a year. Great it was,' said Phil with a mixture of sadness and annoyance.

'Well, it didn't look like it that night. You looked bored with each other, and she kept snapping at you.' Roy tried to make it sound as gentle as possible.

'You can't be up there all the time on some high. We'd have been all right.'

Roy did not answer.

After a time Phil blurted out: 'Stuff it. My best mate. I persuade you to come in as a special 'cause I'm having a good time. I get you along to the do at the police house to meet my girl and wallop. You wouldn't even have met her otherwise.'

'Oh, come on, Phil. Sooner or later you'd have brought her to the rugby club.'

'Maybe,' shrugged Phil.

'In fact, I was surprised you hadn't brought her there before. That's one of the things she said about you.' Roy immediately realised his mistake but carried on. 'You didn't include her in much of your other social life.'

'Oh, yeah? Been slagging me off to you, has she?' shouted Phil.

'No, course not,' protested Roy. Oh, blimey, now it was worse.

He had always enjoyed walking. He reflected on this as he left the road to climb on to the soft grass of the Downs. Walking on turf where there were not too many others reminded him of the time before he was famous. Nobody took any notice of him then. They still didn't, when he was on this sort of terrain; there was nobody much to take notice of him.

Slowly he made his way along the paths separating the lines of bushes. As he came towards the end of them about fifteen minutes later he braced himself. He was coming to another road and more people again. There was a car park, and an ice cream van. He decided he would treat himself to one last ice cream.

He approached the van. There were no other customers about. The man looked up from his paper. He had sold ice cream at this spot for years.

'Yes, sir? What can I do for you?'

The walker asked for a cornet.

'That'll be 40p,' said the vendor and frowned as he wrestled with his memory. He thought he knew the man. 'Lovely afternoon, isn't it?' He gave him the change.

The other nodded and gave a polite 'yes' before walking away. The ice cream seller looked after him as the man moved off towards Beachy Head.

'Where have I seen him before?' he said to himself as he racked his brain.

Phil and Roy were just climbing on to the Downs.

'Yeah, I s'pose you're right,' Phil was saying. 'I didn't want to admit it. But, yes, we *were* getting on each other's nerves.'

Roy started to feel another sort of awkwardness. 'I didn't want it to happen,' he said, 'but it just did. I'm sorry anyway.'

'It's all right,' said his friend. 'How is Mandy anyway? Is she OK?'

'Yes, fine,' said Roy. 'I do like her a lot. But I do want you and me to be mates still.'

'Yeah, course,' answered Phil. 'Look, it's my twenty-first in a fortnight. You're coming, I hope.'

'Course I will. Wouldn't miss that one,' he laughed. 'Then a month or two after that it'll be mine. I'll expect you there. Oh!' His face clouded. 'Mandy'll be at that one.'

'That's all right,' laughed Phil. 'I'll be well over it by then.'

'Oh, come on, Dad. You must know why he was famous. Was he a film star, for instance?'

He laughed. 'No use asking me, love. When do I ever go to the pictures?'

'Pictures!' scoffed Julie. 'They call it the cinema now.'

Julie had just drawn up in her mini. She often came to the ice cream van to give her father some help on weekends. It made a change from the secretarial work she did at the police station during the week. Just as she started again to pump her father, Phil and Roy emerged on the scene.

'Well,' said Julie, 'look who's turned up? Can't I ever get away from you lot?'

'Oh, that's nice, isn't it?' said Roy. 'It's really good to be made to feel welcome.'

'I'll say,' endorsed Phil. 'If you ask me, Roy, we ought to take our custom elsewhere.' They both laughed.

'Well,' observed Julie. 'So you too are talking to each other again, are you?'

The special constables looked awkward. Julie was not noted for her tact.

Phil changed the subject. 'How's business, Mr Palmer?'

'Bit slow,' came the answer. 'Only to be expected before the season gets going. Would you lads like anything, my treat, of course?'

'Oh no, thanks all the same,' said one.

'Best not on duty,' followed up the other.

'Where are you making for, Beachy Head?' asked Mr Palmer.

'Yes,' replied Phil. 'We've been told to walk across that way.'

'You might come across Dad's famous personality,' laughed Julie.

'What's that?' asked Roy.

'Dad reckons he sold a cornet to someone famous about twenty minutes ago, and he can't think who he is.'

'Michael Jackson? offered Phil helpfully.

'Who?' said Mr Palmer.

'Don't bother,' sighed Julie. 'Dad's hopeless on names, even if he recognises them.'

'Well, there are a lot of names in town for the Royal Show at the Congress tonight,' said Roy. 'We're on duty at the front, for Princess Margaret's arrival.'

'Oh, well, have a nice time,' said Julie. 'Get her autograph for me.'

'You must be joking. But that reminds me,' said Roy, 'we'd better get going, Phil.'

'Yes,' answered his colleague, 'there's quite a bit to do.'

'Will I see you both this week?' asked Julie.

'No,' said Phil, 'we're not due on for another ten days or so.' Julie nodded and Phil said, as though the thought had just struck him, 'but it's my twenty-first birthday in a fortnight's time, Julie. The twenty-eighth. Would you like to come?'

'Yes, please,' answered Julie. 'I'll look forward to that.'

Roy smiled to himself. They said their goodbyes.

'Nice lads, those,' said Mr Palmer.

'Yes,' said Julie. 'Especially Phil. You know what he said once? Whenever he has to arrest someone, it always makes him feel sick, taking their liberty away. I've *never* heard anyone in the Force say that before.'

'Well, he won't get far like that,' chuckled Mr Palmer, 'if he's going to feel ill every time.'

'No, I know that,' said Julie, staring after the specials as they walked on. 'I just think it says something about him, that's all. Now then, Dad. This famous person. A sportsman perhaps?'

'I don't know, Julie,' laughed Mr. Palmer. 'You know me. I only follow snooker. And it certainly wasn't Steve Davis.'

'Well, all right,' persisted his daughter. 'You do watch a lot of television. Was it someone on the box?'

'It's funny you say that, because I had the feeling I'd seen him this week.'

'Could have been any night then,' said Julie. 'Your foot was bad every night last week and you were glued in front of the box.'

'That's right,' said her father, glimmers of recognition beginning to percolate through to him. 'It *was* something on television. Oh, now I know who it was. And to think he bought an ice cream off me!'

'Yes, but who was it?' asked an exasperated Julie.

'So . . . ,' chortled Roy gleefully, 'you're not letting too much grass grow under your feet, are you? It's Julie next on the pulling list, eh?'

'Get off,' shrugged Phil. 'We've both worked with her for a while now. It's only an invite to a party.'

'Yeah, yeah,' reassured his friend.

'I'll knock that helmet clean off your head in a minute.'

'We'll both be out of a job if you do,' laughed Roy.

They continued along the road towards Beachy Head, laughing and joking and generally winding each other up.

About twenty minutes later they were close to the cliff top

when a piercing scream stopped them in their tracks. In a moment they saw the elderly lady standing a short distance from the edge. She had just jumped up from the garden chair she had been sitting in. Phil and Roy raced over to her. She saw them coming and started towards them, crying.

'Oh, I saw him. He walked up and down a couple of times. Then he got down and just rolled over the edge,' she said through her tears.

'Shall I go?' said Roy.

'Yes, do that,' answered Phil. 'I'll stay with the lady.'

Roy bounded off to the telephone kiosk to raise the alarm and Phil gently guided the old lady back to her chair. He sat her down and picked up the knitting she had dropped as she stood up. Then he went to the edge. There was no sign of anyone hanging on or caught near the top. He came back to her. She was clearly distressed. He knelt down and put an arm around her shoulders. Phil looked at his watch. It was 2.15. He looked at the area near the old lady's chair.

'You're not alone here, are you, love?'

'No,' she replied, 'my daughter and son-in-law brought me up and settled me here while they went off for a walk. What a terrible thing for someone to do.'

She started sobbing again. A small crowd was now gathering. Phil hugged her closer to him.

'The strange thing is,' she confided, 'I thought I knew him.'

'Did you?' said Phil.

'Oh, I don't mean personally. I mean someone on television or something like that. I couldn't tell you who.'

Phil looked at the people around them. 'Did any of you see the man go over the edge of the cliff just now?'

They all shook their heads. Over the top of them Phil saw Roy running back from the telephone kiosk. In the distance he could hear the sound of the siren and could just make out the familiar sight of a range rover heading towards them from Birling Gap.

'Oh, well,' said Phil, turning back to the old lady, 'marine rescue will be here in a minute. We'll soon know who he was.'

Essex Persons

It was crowded in the bar as it always was on a Friday night. The tensions and claustrophobia of city life were about to be unleashed upon the unsuspecting Acacia Avenues of suburbia, or in Jane's case, the cockle sheds and boating life at Leigh-on-Sea. Not that she would have much time for any of that this particular weekend.

'So I won't see you there on Sunday morning,' said Kate to her friend.

'It's doubtful,' replied Jane. 'Unless I can get through the committee work in time. Beryl will be giving me a hand.'

'Yes, of course,' said the third of the trio being jostled in the noisy pub. 'In fact, if it's all worked out you can leave me with the typing.'

'Thanks,' said Jane, 'We'll see how it goes.'

'Oh, God. This isn't more in the effort to keep Thatcher afloat, is it?' Kate's eyes rolled heavenwards.

'Brace yourself, Beryl, it's coming,' observed Jane.

'Don't worry,' laughed Beryl. 'Remember, I'm used to it too.'

'It's all very well for us as single women,' said Kate. 'But supposing we had husbands and kids. Health and education would suddenly become important. Then the full brunt of Maggie's Britain would really hit us. It's not good enough to be so complacent.'

'I've never been complacent about health and education,' argued Jane. 'I don't suggest we've got it right, but I'm determined we are going in the right direction.'

'The right direction for what, though?' asked Kate.

'Oh, come on,' put in Beryl. 'We've all had a hard week. Let's have another drink. Same again, Kate?'

Kate nodded, but Jane said she was all right with what she

had. Beryl fought her way to the bar through the two-piece suits. She became vaguely aware of a commotion on the far side.

'So what?' slurred the young man, smart and good-looking, wearing all of £400 on his back. He would have looked even better if his self-assured attitude had not taken the edge off it. He had the kind of presence that made him the centre of attention with his city band of followers.

Arnold, at thirty, was the oldest of the group. It was to him that the young man, bleary-eyed with drink, had addressed his question.

'All I'm saying is that you'll burn yourself out by the time you're forty if you carry on like this,' protested Arnold weakly.

'Instead of what? Pushing bits of paper about like you in that boring insurance office until you're sixty? Stuff that!'

Arnold was uneasy. He could not cope with having to defend himself. He wished he had not pursued the matter. He would try and get out of it as quickly as possible.

'Oh, well,' he laughed. 'It's what you want out of life that counts.'

'That's right.' The young man swayed as he wagged a finger stupidly in Arnold's face, a drunken leer widening his mouth. 'And what I want is as much money as I can get. And Arnie, old lad, I'll have more money by the time I'm forty than you'll have by sixty. And I'll pull a sight more birds than you in that time.'

His voice was at fever pitch as he reached the last remark and all his retainers roared with laughter. As Arnold had the star turn's right arm around his shoulders by this time, he too joined in the laughter.

Back at the table that they had just commandeered, Jane and Kate looked round as they caught the general hubbub and resumed their conversation.

'I'm only wondering who I can get to crew for me if you're not available, let alone someone as good as you.'

'Well, look, all right. Beryl says she can take all the typing off my hands, so I'll say I can manage it.'

'Oh, thanks, Jane. I appreciate it.'

'What time do you want me?'

'Half past nine'll be early enough,' said Kate. 'The first race doesn't start till eleven o'clock. That'll be time enough to get the boat ready.'

Beryl returned, without drinks. 'Sorry, Kate. It's so crowded at the bar. I couldn't get through all the city slickers packed in there.'

'Oh, that's OK,' said Kate.

'Time's getting on anyway,' said Jane. 'And I'll be glad to get away from that raucous noise.' She pointed to the other end of the bar.

The three women got up and left the pub. They joined the crowds outside heading up the steps to Fenchurch Street Station just round the corner.

Lots of unsmiling faces, tired after the working week. Year in, year out. What would it all be without Friday night? Back indoors, supper, feet up to watch *Dynasty*. It didn't matter what it was. The aura surrounding it was the ecstasy of Saturday morning, no early rise, no crowds to join on the train.

Jane saw all this in the faces moving in the same direction. She thanked God she did not share their feelings. Every night was Friday night for her, so much to do, so much to be interested in, of which politics played the major part. The local Conservative Association scooped up most of her time, and she revelled in it. Reaching fifty next week would not be a problem. She was blissfully happy to be single and fifty. As she moved up the escalator with her friends she was as contented on this Friday night as she had been the previous Wednesday or the Monday.

'We're well in time for the 5.50,' she said. 'Plenty of space.'

Her two friends agreed. They stepped off the escalator on to the concourse with the surge of people making for the barrier. They moved quickly along the platform and got into the larger of two open compartments that made up the carriage. It was empty so far on this non-stop train to Leigh-on-Sea. The throngs of people just now were veering onto the adjoining platform for the train stopping at more stations.

Back in the pub the young man could not care less either about Friday night. He was fast becoming oblivious to it.

'Listen, Arnie, last year, las' year. . . .'

'Yeah, what about last year, Rick?' encouraged Dave beside him.

Rick leaned against Dave as the effect of the drink brought on the usual sense of camaraderie between men. But Dave was not anything like as drunk.

'Wa-ho. See this!' laughed Dave. 'He's getting cosy with me now.'

The two others roared with laughter. Rick was not amused.

'What are you on about?' he said, still leaning on Dave. 'I'm not a bloody poofter.'

The laughter reached crescendo. People around them started attempting to distance themselves from the group.

'No, course you're not,' said Dave. 'Now what were you going to tell Arnie about last year?'

Rick blinked. 'I've forgotten.'

The laughter swelled again. Arnold looked at his watch. 'I've got to get going,' he said.

'That's right,' said Rick. 'Mother is waiting for little Arnie in Upminster. Din-din's ready.'

Arnold blushed, but he was used to this. He laughed and slid out of the door with a mumbled goodbye, knowing only too well that Rick was right. How would he ever face his mother if he suggested getting married?

'What an arse 'ole!' said Rick, the drink bringing out his true feelings. 'Now then, are you two going to help me out with this lot?'

Dave and the other man laughed as they picked up a crate each of twelve packs from the floor. They carried them out of the door as Rick swayed his way through the bar. Some people laughed. Others breathed a sigh of relief. One or two of the older generation of city workers exchanged observations of disgust at the elements now firmly entrenched in the square mile.

Rick directed his small traffic. 'Come along now, move your arses for this important merchandise,' he bellowed as he led the way for his cronies, brushing people aside, elbowing them out of the way. The people said and did nothing.

'Tories forever,' Rick suddenly yelled at the top of his voice as he clambered up the steps. Dave and the other one roared with laughter again. They continued up the steps laden with their beer packs and moved into the station. Rick continued his chanting.

'Hang 'em and flog 'em and send the black bastards home!'

People tried hard to look away and ignore it all.

On and on the group went, up the escalator, on to the concourse, Rick screaming obscenities, his sidekicks throwing the beer packs about unthinkingly.

'We're in time for the fast,' observed Dave, quickly studying the indicator and the clock.

'The fast it is then,' mouthed Rick.

They were all beyond worrying about fumbling for their season tickets as they pushed through the barrier past a protesting black ticket inspector who received abuse addressed to his pigmentation. Other passengers increased pace in their embarrassment.

They went along the platform a short distance and came to a small open compartment. There was a foursome of seats left on the off-platform side. The three men slid into it. Rick flopped into the seat by the window facing the engine. Dave and the other one dropped the beer packs on the floor at Rick's feet. Dave sat next to Rick and the third man sat opposite Dave who delivered a loud and arrogant belch. Evening newspapers rustled sharply around them.

The guard had already blown the whistle when a man hurled the door open and dived in. He was in his fifties, puffing and panting. He had clearly rushed in and not seen where he was heading. He had a lighted cigarette between his fingers. Rick planted his feet firmly on the clean upholstery opposite him and roared at the man.

'What the hell are you doing with that cigarette? Can't you read? This is a non-smoker.'

The man went red with embarrassment, looked up at the No Smoking sign and quickly extinguished his cigarette. He even said sorry. Rick was not interested in any apology as he reached down for another can of beer.

'Bloody manners of some people,' he said, as the train started moving, and he wiped his shoes back and forth over the upholstery. 'No consideration for people's feelings. I don't want smoke down my lungs.'

The man screwed his eyes deeper into the newspaper he had just unfolded, very nearly piercing two holes through the print.

A young woman got up and went through the interconnecting door to the next compartment. She found a seat behind the foursome of seats where Jane's group was sitting.

'So it's the usual procedure, is it?' queried Beryl.

'Yes, we'll hear the tape and then ask for discussion,' replied Jane.

'It's a bit same-y, isn't it?' suggested Beryl.

'Yes, I get a bit fed up with it,' said Jane, 'listening to this disembodied voice putting over a case we've heard about so many times through the press. But I gather tonight's tape is good, and Chris Patten tries to make it more interesting. In any case it's the discussion about it afterwards that I enjoy so much.'

'Yes, but do you think our old dodderers are going to contribute much to the Green Bill?'

'Well, we'll have to work up what interest we can in it,' said Jane with some excitement. 'It's so new and hopeful. And we ought to be in the forefront of conserving everything. If we can drum up interest locally we'll have more chance of getting the recycling plant established in the area.'

'That's true,' said Beryl. 'I'd certainly like to see this paper on green issues getting wide support.'

'And not before time.' Kate looked up from her book. 'It's taken interest from all other parties for your lot to show any yourselves.'

'Ah, but we haven't made a meal of it before,' said Jane. 'I'm old enough to remember the Clean Air Act. The Tories brought that in over thirty years ago, long before anybody thought of the environment as a subject.'

Kate sighed at Jane's comment and went back to her book.

Jane and Beryl exchanged looks and Jane said, 'I'm hoping to do something about this old dodderer image. I want to see a younger element taking more interest.'

'Not the Young Cons,' said Beryl and winced. 'You remember how they carried on last election night?'

'Don't remind me,' said Jane. 'No, I don't mean that scatty bunch of eighteen-year-olds. I want to see more mature, early-middle-aged people taking part in the political discussion group. In fact we've got a chap coming along tonight. He phoned me last night and said he'd like to join us.'

The train was just speeding through Barking as the man

who had boarded the train with the cigarette stepped into the compartment looking distressed. He found a seat nearby.

All three women looked up at him as Beryl asked, 'Oh, really? What's his name?'

'Chap called Rick Malling,' came the reply.

In the other compartment the atmosphere had reached a low ebb. Rick was now paralytic.

'What for Chrissake made you do that?' Dave was asking. 'Did you hear that, Pete?' he said to the man opposite him.

'Yeah,' laughed Pete. 'Well, why, Rick? What the hell do you want to join the Tories for?'

'Listen!' Rick's mouth could scarcely find shape for the words to be formed. His friends were not far behind as they both stretched down for more beer. Rick carried on.

'The Tories provide the – hic – backbone of this country. They're the only lot what, I mean, who . . .'

The others roared at his tangle of grammar.

'No, listen, you shit bags, they're the only lot who can keep the spades and poofters in their place.'

'Oh, yeah?' leered Dave. 'You sayin' there's no queers in the Tory Party? What about the bloke in Billericay?'

'Ah, yeah,' hiccupped Rick. 'But they got rid of 'im, didn't they? That's . . . just my point. They get, I mean, keep the poofters right in their place.'

'Yeah, but what else? You're not joining the Tories 'cause of that! Surely!'

'No, of course not,' mouthed Rick. 'I want this good life I've got to keep going.'

Dave and Pete laughed. 'Too right.'

'That's reminded me,' said Rick, screwing up his eyes to recall something. 'I've remembered now what I was going to tell that arse 'ole, Arnie. Wouldn't be surprised if he's a poofter hisself.'

Dave laughed. 'You were going to tell him that?'

'No, no, you're twisting everything I say,' protested Rick. 'I was going to tell him about last year. That was it. I was going to tell him that last year I picked up £70,000. £70,000! That dickhead'll never earn that kind of money in his insurance company.'

'No, course he won't,' chipped in Pete. 'But no one picks up the sort of money we do on the stock market. But not many have the pressures either, I shouldn't fink.'

'Jesus, no,' put in Dave. 'But Arnie is right, I reckon. We'll burn ourselves out by the time we're forty. I couldn't go on like that for the rest of my working life.'

'All the more reason to pick up what we can now,' said Rick. '£70,000 last year. It's going to be more than £100,000 this year. That's why I'm joining the Tories. We'll never have this chance if Labour gets in next time.'

'S'pose not,' said Dave. 'So you're going tonight, are you?'

'Yeah,' replied Rick. 'I phoned the secretary of our ward last night. Jane Dixon I think she said her name was. She suggested I go along tonight. There's all various groups apparently, and this one's the political discussion group. I'm not too interested in getting into the thick of all that, not the actual politics crap. But I thought I'd better show willing.'

'You'll be more interested in the crumpet,' laughed Pete. 'But you're a bit old for the Young Conservatives, aren't you?'

'Daresay,' came the reply. 'But they're tasty, some of those girls, from what I've heard. I reckon I can make myself known to a few of them. Shouldn't be too much bother to get them away from the Hoorays.'

'Aren't too many of them now in the Tories,' observed Dave. 'Not like the old toffs. Probably all estate agents and second-hand car dealers, like our bunch at work.'

They all laughed.

'Yes,' agreed Rick. 'The Big Bang did wonders for us.'

'Anyway,' said Dave. 'What about this Jane you spoke to? What she sound like?'

'Rich kind of silky voice,' said Rick. 'Sounded about thirty. Just about my handwriting. Don't mind making a start with her.'

'Except how d'you think you're going to cope with her and a political meeting tonight with the state you're in?' This from Pete.

'Ah, no problem. It's not till 8.30. I'll have a shower when I get in, and a ton of black coffee. You know what I'm like. Never takes me long to sober up.'

He belched loudly again and reached down for another can of beer.

A third passenger folded his newspaper angrily and got up. He walked into the other compartment where Kate had put her book down.

'Now let's get this straight,' Kate was saying. 'You're going to listen to a tape recorded by Chris Patten. Then you'll discuss it and send him a report about what you all think?'

'That's the way it works,' agreed Jane.

'Well, what a waste of time! What chance will there be of his paying attention to it?' asked Kate incredulously.

'Every chance,' protested Jane. 'They get reports in from all over the country and study them. All the local constituencies send in reports.'

'But what notice do they take? Their minds are already made up,' said Kate with growing wonder.

'No, Kate, that's not true. You remember the Shop Trading Act a few years ago?'

'When they were trying to get shops to be able to open on Sundays?'

'Yes. Well, there was tremendous opposition from many of the constituencies. I argued long and hard about the shop workers needing Sundays off if they wanted them. I said there wouldn't be any safeguards for them under the Bill. A lot of people said the same. The Bill was abandoned. So it wasn't just the Opposition. It was our own side as well.'

'Hm. Doesn't seem to have worked with the Poll Tax, does it?'

'No, but we'll keep trying,' said Jane. 'I don't like that either, not the way it's working out.'

Kate sat back and watched as yet another irate passenger came through the interconnecting door to find a seat. Kate frowned and wondered why there was so much movement. Then she looked out of the window to see the train speeding through Upminster.

'Where are we?' Rick's eyes were now closing in on each other.

Dave looked out. 'Just going through Upminster.'

'Oh, Arnie will soon be safe in the bosom of his mother if this is Upminster.'

'Well, there'll be something wrong if he's in his mother's bosom,' said Pete.

They roared with laughter.

'In Arnie's case I bet it's true,' said Rick.

Another laugh.

'Listen,' said Dave. 'If you've made a hundred gees already this year, what are you going to do with it?'

'Well, I'm certainly not going to give it away. No, it's going to be invested for the future.'

'So Terry Wogan's appeal tonight isn't going to see any of your money,' laughed Pete.

'Stuff that,' answered Rick. 'Children in Need? Do me a favour. They picked up £20 million last year. No, I leave all that to the mugs.'

'I want very much,' Jane was saying to Beryl in the other compartment, 'to put the spotlight on giving. I want to get a campaign moving. We've got the interest going over the Children in Need appeal. We had a lot of volunteers come forward for tomorrow's collections. I want to extend that further. Not just this weekend but all the year round.'

'Yes,' agreed Beryl. 'A lot of people in our area are doing all right now. I'm sure they'd have the means, a lot of them.'

Kate scoffed. 'People's willingness to give is in inverse proportion to their ability.'

'Rubbish,' said Jane. 'That's never been true in my experience. Whenever I've had more money I've given more. It's obvious many feel the same way. Last year over one and a half billion pounds were given to charity. People couldn't possibly do that if they hadn't earned the money to give.'

'So how are you going to set about this crusade?' asked Kate, a touch of sarcasm creeping in.

'All sorts of ways. I want to establish a subcommittee to look into it. Get the Rotarians involved perhaps. That's where I want to get the younger element involved in fund-raising activities for the hospitals. In fact I intend to tackle this chap Rick Malling about it tonight.'

'As long as he's energetic enough,' said Beryl.

'I should think he must be to stand the pace of the Stock Exchange these days,' said Jane.

'Real Essex Man!' observed Kate. 'Stock Market vulture, Tory Party. It all fits in.'

Jane refused to be goaded and kept her voice on an even keel. 'You do categorise people, Kate. I'm surprised you haven't used the word "yuppie" yet. Or is that going out of fashion now, like "Sloane"?'

Kate pursed her lips and smiled.

'He sounded a very reasonable chap, as a matter of fact,' continued Jane. 'About twenty-five to thirty, I should think. Sounded rather dishy, I thought.'

'So that's why she's so keen to get him involved,' laughed Kate. 'Too old for the Young Cons, so Jane can home in on him.'

Beryl chuckled and Jane made a face.

'He sounds a perfectly ordinary young chap with an interest in politics. I'm sure he's got a sense of responsibility and will respond to an appeal to undertake money-raising activities for good causes.'

As Jane spoke, a distressed young woman rushed into the compartment through the interconnecting door. She was crying as she surveyed the vomit on the front of her dress.

Jane jumped up. 'Oh dear. You're ill!'

'No, it's not me,' the woman cried. 'It's some man in the next compartment. He's being disgusting with his friends, getting drunker by the minute. I asked him to stop shouting and swearing and he got up and came over to me. I thought he was going to hit me. Instead of that he was sick all over me.'

Jane felt the blood rushing to her head. 'Didn't anyone else say anything?'

The girl shook her head.

Jane asked Kate to take care of her, and then her sudden temper propelled her through the interconnecting doors closely followed by Beryl.

Rick's two friends were sitting down sheepishly, surveying the mess on the seat where the girl had been sitting, and the floor close by. Jane then saw Rick leaning out of the window, clearly continuing to empty his stomach. As Jane drew closer he leaned up. He stood there swaying in motion with the train as it sped through Basildon. Beer cans were strewn all about. Jane was in a fury.

'You filthy oaf,' she screamed at Rick. 'What sort of behaviour do you call this?'

'Fuck off, you,' Rick slurred. 'Don't need any lecture from you.'

'You need it from someone,' yelled Jane. 'What gives you the right to do all this, cause distress to people? Haven't you got any consideration for others?'

'No,' laughed Rick, 'I have to spend too much time considering myself.'

Dave and Pete half laughed with him.

'You bloody moron,' shouted Jane.

'Oh, swearing now, are we? Not very ladylike.'

Before Jane realised it, Rick lunged at her and took a powerful swing. Jane was immediately off-balance with the blow and the swaying of the train as it hurtled along the banked curve at Pitsea. She knew nothing of the impact as she crashed down and her head connected with the door at the end of the compartment. She lay quite still.

Beryl rushed over, distressed that her friend was unconscious. But after a second or two she saw the blood oozing from her left ear. Kate emerged through the interconnecting door in time to hear Beryl's piercing scream.

Going to Extremes

Pauline winced as she clambered on to the train. Arthritis was beginning to take its toll on her small frame. She struggled through the narrow corridor, peering into the separate compartments. She relaxed as she saw a near-full compartment of women and slid back the door.

Conversation stopped as they looked up to see the small figure in a yellow woollen hat stretched down hard on her head. Their own hats were rather more upmarket.

'Is there room for one more?' asked Pauline.

Murmurs of assent in varying degrees of tolerance provided the answer. She stepped gingerly through a minefield of court shoes to the window seat still vacant.

The conversation continued, though on a more tentative basis. The group had felt sure that in taking up five of the six seats available in the compartment they would be left to themselves. The sudden intrusion ought not to have inhibited discussion, but it was doing so. The well-dressed ladies were also distracted by the big noisy bag the newcomer was fiddling about with and diving into after she had sorted herself out in her seat.

Pauline looked up to find one or two watching her. Undaunted, she met their looks with a squinting smile and slight raising of her small shoulders. She felt entirely at ease. The ladies looked awkward in returning the smile and tried to absorb themselves again.

'Ee, I don't know, Hilda,' said one. 'That there motion you got through at Lytham last year was all very well. But you can't expect traders to go so far.'

'Well, think on 't,' replied Hilda. 'There's no point in expressing belief in the environment and not acting on 't.'

'Well, what about my Harry's shop, for instance?' the woman protested. 'What's supposed to happen to all his stock of CFC cans? Does he just dump them and lose all that money?'

'I know it's difficult,' said Hilda. 'But there comes a time when we have to put money where our mouths are.'

'Hm!' sniffed the other. 'It's all very well for folks like thee to talk, Hilda Vernon. It's not thy money at stake.'

'I appreciate that, Mavis. I do, really. But the conference does want to see evidence of what we're doing. Perhaps your Harry could make a start by not ordering any more goods that are unfriendly to the environment.'

Another sniff from Mavis. 'I don't know about that. Harry's very set in his ways.'

'Excuse me.'

The five ladies looked startled at the sudden interruption. Pauline was not in the least perturbed that she had gained their full attention.

'Are you going as far as Northslade?'

'Aye, that's right,' replied Mavis, sitting opposite her. There was a certain abruptness in her tone.

By contrast Hilda smiled. She was sitting next to Pauline. Intrigued by the reading material on her lap, she asked Pauline where she was going.

'Oh, to Northslade as well. To the Glenister Arts Theatre.'

'Oh aye, that's next to the conference hall where we're all going.'

After the pause that followed, Hilda asked, 'Do you know Northslade well then?'

'Not a great deal. But I've been to the theatre sixteen times in the last three years.'

'Good Heavens!' exclaimed Hilda. 'That's a long way to travel to a theatre. You must have seen a lot of different plays there.'

'Oh no,' replied Pauline, 'just the one thing, *The Minstrel Years*.'

'That's the offshoot of the old *Black and White Minstrel Show*, isn't it?' said Hilda.

'That's right,' came the enthusiastic reply. 'I saw it 568 times at the Victoria Palace.'

Mavis gasped. 'Whatever for?'

Pauline laughed. 'I liked being there. Two or three times a week. It was like a way of life.'

'I can see that from all those books you've got there,' observed Hilda. 'I didn't know so much was published about them.'

'Some of it I made up in my own folders, from articles, that sort of thing. But look at this magazine. It gives you a history of every member of the cast and what happened to them after the show finished. Go on, choose a name and I'll tell you what happened to him.'

'Well, perhaps not just now, if you don't mind,' smiled Hilda awkwardly.

Mavis found difficulty in containing herself. 'Didn't you get bored with it after a while? Seeing same show week in, week out?'

'Good gracious, no,' cried Pauline. 'Bored? Bored? The very last thing!'

'But you were hearing the same songs over and over. There was nowt new.'

'Oh, that didn't matter. It was the atmosphere.' Pauline shrugged and laughed. 'Besides, all those years in London, I didn't really know anybody. There was nothing else to do.'

For a moment Pauline allowed the smile to fall from her face. The compartment went suddenly quiet.

The silence was broken by Hilda. 'Come on then, love. Give us your magazine and I'll pick a name.'

Pauline's face was aglow once more as she pushed the magazine into Hilda's hands, which quickly manipulated the pages until they stayed firm about halfway through the publication.

'Here's one,' said Hilda, 'Terry Crispin!'

Pauline pounced on it straightaway. 'Terry was with us until 1970. Then he married one of the dancers. Do you remember, they were the Television Toppers?'

The compartment nodded.

'They left the business and went up to Scotland to open a hotel.'

'Absolutely right,' said Hilda.

'They still send me a Christmas card,' said Pauline eagerly. 'Got two daughters now. Lovely family. Go on, give me another one.'

'All right then. Just one more.' Hilda was sympathetic but

she was determined not to spend the next couple of hours being a quiz master. She thumbed through and set upon a name and Pauline gave her the history of the artist and was proved right. Hilda said 'very good' and firmly returned the magazine to the owner. But she was kind enough not to dismiss the subject straightaway.

'So you obviously keep up with them even now.'

'Oh yes,' said Pauline, warming up. 'I was overjoyed when my favourite formed a minstrel company again four years ago.'

Mavis was getting a bit exasperated. 'Who's yer favourite then?'

'Ronny Wilkinson.' Pauline's eyes positively glazed over. 'He was always special. Carried on doing his act long after the TV show finished. Then four years ago he decided to start up a minstrel company of his own. Managed to get some of the originals back. They'd left the business long since. Brought them out of retirement, he did. Well, of course, Ronny himself is sixty-four now.'

One of the other ladies spoke for the first time, the one sitting the other side of Mavis.

'I always liked watching the show of a Saturday night. Never could understand why they took it off. It were so popular. Perhaps they'll bring it back.'

'Oh, he's a lovely chap,' Pauline continued as though the woman had not spoken. 'And he thinks the world of me, you know. I've followed him around all these years. Gone to all the theatres he's appeared at. Often had tea with him before the show or seen him in his dressing room afterwards.'

Pauline's face inclined towards theirs and they responded, involuntarily. It was as though she was about to impart something in the strictest confidence.

'He said to me once that I was his greatest fan.'

The ladies moved their heads back to their former positions. Mavis allowed herself a deep sigh as she looked out of the window and saw that the train was just pulling in to Preston. It would be ages before they reached Northslade.

Ronny Wilkinson was making steady if morose progress along the M6.

'I don't know. It's times like this I envy the likes of Terry Crispin, getting out of it and going to Scotland to his hotel.'

His listener took a deep breath. He stretched his arms as far as the minibus roof would allow. He looked round to see the other three dozing. He yawned and rubbed his eyes.

'Yeah, he did all right for himself, that lad. Married the best-looking bird in the chorus for cover and gathered all those young waiters round him.'

Ronny laughed bitterly. 'Shrewd buggers, those sort of poofters. I'll say that for them. Where are we now, Len?'

Leonard Suffolk consulted the map in front of him.

'About twenty-five miles from Preston. I'll take over from there if you like.'

'OK. They all asleep in the back?'

'Yeah,' said Len. 'Our young pianist friend is nearly snoring. Not surprised.' He lowered his voice. 'All that catching up to do after last night.'

Ronny let out a cynical chuckle. 'He does seem to be determined when he's made his mind up.'

Len looked round again. 'Seems to have cracked it this time. Patsy's got her arms round him like she's holding on to a cliff edge.'

Ronny laughed again. 'Some of these young dancers, mate. They get so smitten with their first whiff of show business after dancing school.'

'Yeah,' yawned Len. 'What about you? Scored yet with one of the girls?'

'Can't be bothered now. Bloody sixty-five this month. I ought to be packing it all in. All this nonsense. Driving endless miles round the country to play in some heartless new arts centre in front of less than a hundred.'

'Know what you mean. No atmosphere in these places. Are you really coming up to sixty-five, Ron?'

'Yes, in a couple of weeks,' replied Ronny.

'I'm only two years behind you,' Len laughed. 'Does seem bloody ridiculous, doesn't it? The likes of us cavorting around the country blacking our faces up and singing the same old songs!'

'Speak for yourself,' said Ronny. 'If you changed your act once in a while, maybe you wouldn't be so bored.'

'Cheeky bugger,' said his long-time colleague.

'I take a leaf out of my old Dad's book. He once said to me that before the First World War, he could go around every theatre in the country with the same routine and it would take him seven years to do it.'

'Don't know how he'd get on today, with less than half the theatres left, and television to soak up your material in three minutes.'

Len sighed and looked out of the window as the motorway droned on. He gazed at the map in front of him.

'Should be about another couple of hours to Northslade. That place is getting to be a regular feature.'

'Yes,' answered Ronny. 'I did have hopes for a summer season next year. Very much in the balance now with a change of council.'

'Oh God, are we political up there now?' Len pulled himself up to sit straight in the seat.

'Seems so. Letter arrived in the office last week from the theatres division chief. Jumped up little sod. Never has liked us. Now he's got political muscle behind him, he's lapping it up.'

'What did it say then, Ron?'

Ronny pointed Len Suffolk to the glove compartment. Len reached in and unfolded the letter headed: Northslade Borough Council. He read the short message:

The Council notes that your booking for the Glenister Arts Theatre was made several months ago, and it is prepared to honour its commitment to you. However, the Council wishes you to note that your company is not welcome here. The change in its political composition since the time of your booking renders the Council unsympathetic to your kind of performance which is not conducive to good taste.

Len folded the paper and threw it back into the glove compartment in disgust.

'Huh! All that crap they put on the rest of the year with everybody screaming four-letter words at each other. Is that what they call good taste?'

'Bloody hypocrites, the lot of them,' echoed Ronny.

84

'What with all that and having to face Pauline.'

Len laughed. 'Pauline! The one and only Ronny Wilkinson groupie!'

'She's been following me around for twenty years now. More than that,' remembered Ronny. 'Insisted on a new photo every performance. She must have bloody thousands by now.'

'Must be obsession, mustn't it? No sane person would carry on like that,' observed Len.

'Gets on my bloody nerves,' said Ronny. 'She's like a leech. All of it reflected glory. She probably hands around the latest photo I give her to everyone she meets.'

Ronny continued to speak contemptuously of Pauline. He shuddered to think that they had known each other when both were fairly young. Now they were both old, like a married couple, though he had been forced into the marriage. The things one had to put up with. Live by the public and you have to die by the public.

'It must come down to loneliness in the end,' said Len.

'Course it does,' agreed Ronny. 'But I resent her working out her bloody emotions on my performance. It's only a job after all. She wouldn't swoon over a bank manager going over his accounts. She wouldn't hand him a fresh rose in an envelope as he walked into his office every morning.'

Len laughed. 'I notice the way you practically ignore her now every time you run into her.'

'It's the only thing I can do, but she never takes the hint. Here, let's go into this services for a coffee and you can take over.'

Harry Graham was proving a popular Mayor of Northslade. People warmed to his jovial smile and big frame. He lapped up their affection and he was very contented with the world as he drove along the seafront to the Glenister Arts Theatre.

His seventeen-year-old son sitting beside him could not feel quite the same contentment. On this, the first morning of his Youth Training Scheme position at the theatre, Kevin was clearly apprehensive. His father spotted it.

'Now don't you worry about a thing,' said Mayor Graham. 'You've met them all now, haven't you?'

Kevin nodded and chanced a smile.

'Well then. And remember, I shall only be next door this morning if you want me.'

Kevin smiled even more at the irony of interrupting his father in the middle of some public function or other. But he used the opportunity to take his mind off his apprehension.

'What have you got on today then, Dad?'

'Speech of welcome in the conference hall,' replied his father, 'for the Women's Institute North West convention.'

'Sounds exciting,' said Kevin ironically.

'Don't knock it, boy. I shall be the only man in a hall of eight hundred people.'

He let out a great roar of laughter and slapped his son's right thigh. Kevin grinned and looked out of the window, knowing what a joke it was. Ma and Pa were devoted to each other.

The Mayor turned off the seafront to the theatre, dropped his son off at the stage door and wished him luck. Then he drove the short distance to the town hall and parked his car. He walked to his office and found his chauffeur waiting outside.

'Won't be long, Fred,' he said cheerily to the driver and looked in on his secretary. There were a couple of matters that needed discussion but he soon emerged and went with the driver out to the official car waiting by the town hall steps. Within seconds the car glided away and arrived a few minutes later at the conference hall, just around the corner from where the Mayor had left his son a matter of twenty minutes before.

The car pulled up, the chauffeur got out quickly, but Harry Graham was already opening his door to be greeted by a woman in an enormous hat.

The Mayor thrust his hand forward. 'You must be Mrs Beaminster,' he smiled broadly.

The woman was overjoyed that the Mayor should actually know the name of the president of the W.I. North West section. She was won over instantly by Harry Graham and she led him into the foyer.

As the official car was drawing away, a group of women emerged on the scene.

'My goodness,' said Pauline. 'Looks like a big occasion. That was the Mayor's car, wasn't it?'

'Aye,' said Mavis. 'It's always a big function is our convention oop here. Wherever it's held, Mayor always comes.'

'Well, this is where we part company.' Pauline gave a self-conscious half-laugh.

'Yes,' came an equal half-laugh from Hilda, who could not help noticing the general sigh of relief coming from the rest of the group. It had been a long rail journey as Pauline has warmed to her theme increasingly. They had had Ronny Wilkinson to the back teeth. But Hilda felt pity for her more than anything else.

'Well, you'll be getting off to your boarding house now and mebbe having a rest before the show tonight.'

'Oh no, I shall get to the theatre as soon as I can,' said Pauline. 'I always get there before Ronny arrives. Thank you again for helping me to choose the right dress for the occasion. I brought the two because I really wasn't sure. You see, Ronny has always said he likes me very much in both dresses. I keep asking him which one he likes best but he'll never tell me. He always says he likes them both equally. Wasn't it lucky there was a toilet so close to our compartment? I was able to change so quickly so that you could see both dresses.'

Mavis shuddered as she recalled again the unexpected fashion show they had been treated to on the train.

Pauline thanked them again and said goodbye. Hilda told her to have a good time but the wish was not reciprocated. Pauline had no room in her head to consider the Women's Institute convention as she set off towards her guesthouse near the theatre, oblivious to everything else.

Mavis let rip. 'Oh God, I don't believe we've got rid of her at last.' There were several echoes.

'Now, now, all of you,' protested Hilda. 'Think yourselves lucky that you're nowt so lonely as she is. It's only been a couple of hours for us on train.'

'Yes, you're quite right, Hilda,' said one of the others. 'Let's hope she has a good time tonight.'

Mavis was not in the mood. 'Come on,' she said abruptly. 'It's nearly twelve o'clock. The opening address'll be starting soon.'

The ladies joined the remaining delegates hurrying into the hall.

While the Mayor was welcoming the packed convention to

Northslade and wishing them a pleasant stay in the town, the Deputy Mayor was just leaving the town hall with two councillors. On the steps they were joined by an assortment of people, some carrying placards.

'Right, Julie,' said the deputy to a woman at the front of the group. 'We'll have to move off in two's or three's as we haven't involved the police. Afraid I wasn't able to drum up more support from the councillors. Typical, when you ask people to put their money where their mouths are!'

'It's a start anyway,' replied Julie. 'I don't s'pose this town has ever seen a demo of any sort before.'

The Deputy Mayor laughed. 'Too right. I've lived in the place most of my life and usually found it difficult to get folk worked up much about issues. Still, if you want to get your folks organised, we'll follow up behind a few paces.'

'OK,' said Julie and went across to the dozen or so people gathered. She took a placard and moved off with two others. At intervals of three minutes, the rest did the same. There were two left at the rear and shortly after they began walking, the Deputy Mayor and the two councillors followed on.

In the town centre the elderly clutched hold of their shopping trolleys that acted as walking aids and peered through their rheumy eyes at the placards. The less elderly saw the messages more clearly. At intervals of two or three minutes they read such entreaties as: Don't go to the racist minstrel show at the theatre this week.

A married couple doing their shopping had not known the show would be appearing in the town.

'Look at that,' said the wife. 'Remember how we loved them on television. There's a poster advertising them. They're on this week at the Glenister.'

'Oh well, let's go and see them, dear,' said the husband.

The fragmented group soldiered on with their signs: Black make-up on whites demeans the blacks: Down with stereotypes: No platform for racists.

Seeing the first two signs, people waited to see if there were any others, as though watching an impromptu parade. Depending on their political beliefs they either sighed in frustration or felt a surge of approval.

Nobody took any notice of the Deputy Mayor or the councillors, who were ordinarily dressed by contrast to the others and did not carry any placards.

They made their way slowly out of the town centre down to the seafront to pass along the promenade of early summer holidaymakers taking advantage of the warm sun. They glanced up cursorily from their deckchairs and tabloids and returned as quickly to their contentment.

The group's collective progress eventually brought them to the front of the Glenister Arts Theatre. In accordance with their arrangements half of their number, together with one of the councillors, stayed put while the rest went round the corner and along the road to the stage door. The Deputy Mayor had decided to move at will to cover both picket lines.

The theatre manager emerged at that moment. He recognised the man in front of him from several civic occasions at the theatre. He also took in the general situation instantly.

'Hello, Jim,' the manager greeted the Deputy Mayor. 'How are you?'

'Fine, thanks, Terry. And yourself?'

'Well, I was just on my way home for a break before tonight's customers start arriving. Seeing all of you here makes me wonder whether I should go.'

'Well, there's no need to stay on our account. We're not here to cause trouble.'

'So what *are* you here for?' asked the theatre manager in a sympathetic tone.

'Purely as a peaceful protest and no more,' replied the Deputy Mayor.

'Hm, I don't know.' The theatre manager hesitated. 'Presumably you're going to speak to people as they come to make bookings?'

'Not necessarily,' replied the Deputy Mayor. 'It's more likely they'll speak to us. If any of us speaks first and the person concerned isn't interested in listening, we won't push it.'

'Can still be regarded as intimidation, though,' said the manager, with increasing doubt.

'Oh come on, Terry. It's only people talking to one another. If they're not interested, they don't have to answer.'

Terry Conrad glanced over the small group. 'Is this all of you, Jim?'

'No, we've got the same number at the stage door.'

Terry's eyes widened a little. He checked his watch. Ronny Wilkinson would be turning up soon, and already the scenery dock next to the stage door was busy with the company's lorry that had just arrived.

'I'll take a look round there,' said Terry, and the Deputy Mayor went with him.

'I would have liked some warning of this, Jim,' he said as they headed around the corner. 'I didn't see anything in the local paper.'

'We were just too late for the deadline. We only decided to do this on Friday.'

Terry Conrad felt some sympathy with the cause. At the age of forty, he had spent more than half his life in the theatre and had only moved on to the management side in the last year or two. He had got used to the idea of playing Romeo opposite a black Juliet and, as far as he recalled, nobody had even commented on the fact. The idea of white men slapping mud packs of black paint on their faces to look like negroes of the old South did not annoy him so much as make him feel uncomfortable. But he was determined to keep the peace.

In the scenery dock there was plenty of activity. Tony Hawton, the young stage manager, stood by the side of the dock and surveyed the scene, a trifle apprehensively. He was as surprised as the theatre manager to be confronted by a demonstration with placards. He watched carefully as his small band of workers making up the stage crew carted the scenery and props from the lorry to the dock door leading on to the stage. He was especially conscious of his newly arrived YTS lad, the Mayor's son. As the boy came past him to go to the lorry and thus run the gauntlet of the demonstration again, Tony called him over.

'Hey, Kevin. Here a minute. Look, perhaps it would be a good idea if you stayed inside and sat this one out. There isn't much to do.'

'I'm OK, thank you,' said Kevin enthusiastically and wondered why the stage manager was excusing him. He had only been there for an hour or so.

Tony cleared his throat. 'Well, er, this is your first day, and none of us was expecting this demo, and er, well, you're a bit young if anything happens.'

The confident boy grinned. 'Oh, that's all right, Tony. I've taken a judo course and I'm doing karate now. I can handle myself all right.'

'I'm sure you can, Kevin. But after all,' he hesitated, 'you are the Mayor's son.'

The boy's infectious smile spread over his face again. 'Well, if that's what you're worried about, I'll certainly carry on. Dad's been insistent all along that I don't get any special privileges while he's in office.'

'Well, all right,' relented Tony Hawton uneasily.

'I'm surprised, though,' said Kevin as he continued towards the lorry, 'that my Dad didn't warn me about it.'

By now the theatre manager and the Deputy Mayor had arrived on the scene.

'Everything all right, Tony?' queried Terry Conrad.

'Yes, fine so far,' answered the stage manager. 'But I'd like to know if there'll be any more demonstrators showing up.'

The Deputy Mayor confirmed that there would not be. The theatre manager told him of the others at the entrance to the theatre but that they would be staying there.

'We're OK then,' said Tony. 'In any case it looks as though we'll only be another quarter of an hour, then we'll be inside working.'

'In that case, Jim,' said the theatre manager, somewhat reassured, 'I'll leave you to it.'

The Deputy Mayor shook hands with Terry Conrad and the latter walked back to the front of the theatre to collect his car.

Ten minutes later, the stage manager breathed a sigh of relief as the lorry drove off and he was able to pull down the shutter of the scenery dock. He scarcely gave the demonstrators a glance as he disappeared from view.

As the shutter came down, the group saw a little old lady totter towards them, set a small fold-up canvas stool in place and sit down next to them by the stage door. She looked up at them and smiled.

'Waiting for their autographs, are you?' asked Pauline confidently. She was oblivious to the placards held aloft.

'Er, no,' said a young woman, 'nothing like that.'

'Oh, well,' smiled Pauline, 'I expect you just want to catch a glimpse of them when they arrive. I know what it's like. I was stagestruck when I was young like you.'

The woman looked at her friend, confused, and then at the councillor who winked.

'Course I got over all that long ago Ronny's a friend now not an object of hero worship he'd be very disappointed and wonder what had happened if he didn't find me waiting for him at the stage door when he arrived anywhere now we've got quite a long wait ahead of us he doesn't usually get here until 3 o'clock or so might as well get settled until he comes he drives a minibus you know brings some of the company with him Leonard Suffolk and people like that.'

Pauline drew breath and looked up at the young woman. 'Are you from around these parts or have you travelled a long way to see the show?'

'Oh, Jesus, no, she's there already sitting on that bloody stool.'

Ronny Wilkinson's jaw dropped a mile as Len Suffolk turned the corner and steered the minibus to the stage door.

'Yes, but even worse, look what's beyond her,' observed Len.

Ronny let out a profanity as the small group of people and the placards came into view.

The dancers and the pianist in the back looked worried as Len brought the minibus to a halt. As they slowly extricated themselves from the vehicle, the chanting started.

'No racist minstrel shows in Northslade, no racist minstrel shows in Northslade.'

Ronny Wilkinson was ready for Councillor Parkin who was approaching him.

'Mr Wilkinson?' he queried.

The other nodded.

'Did you receive our letter?' asked the councillor.

'Yes,' answered Ronny abruptly.

'There's nothing personal in this, but we feel very strongly about your type of show.'

'Yes, yes, I've heard it all before. It's because of people like you we're no longer in the West End or on television. Have you any idea of the number of livelihoods you've ditched because of your so-called progressive attitudes?' Ronny was fuming.

'That's as may be,' came the reply, 'but I'm sure you could all channel your talents into something more savoury.'

'Not to equal the success we all had with this format,' said an embittered Ronny.

'So, it doesn't matter who you upset as long as you're successful!' This from the Deputy Mayor who had just returned to the scene, this time with a local news reporter and a photographer in tow. They went to work immediately and hungrily.

'You people talk such rubbish about this racist crap.' Ronny's face was getting redder as he started to take on two of them. He could feel the hostility from the pickets growing. Leonard Suffolk was beside him, but the dancers and the young pianist had already scuttled in through the stage door.

'We are simply a group of people singing some old songs that people like,' continued Ronny.

'And dressed up as black people!' declared the Deputy Mayor.

'So what the hell's wrong with that?' This from Leonard Suffolk. 'We don't say or sing anything racist or make nasty comments. Certainly no jokes about them.'

'No, you just insult them by dressing up like them, making them look like caricatures,' Julie, the spokesperson of the group, now joined in.

'You people talk bloody wet,' Ronny said, now raising his voice. He had had a long drive from London and he felt he could do without this. 'You're so hypersensitive. What about an actor portraying a Frenchman? Does he insult him by putting on an accent?'

'If he's attempting to ridicule, certainly he does.'

'Ridicule, is it?' snorted Ronny. 'Some of our songs are the negro spirituals of old. If you bothered to come to see the show, so you knew what you were talking about, you'd hear some of those songs which pay recognition to the suffering of the blacks.'

'While at the same time dressing up like the golliwogs we used to get on jam pots,' the Deputy Mayor said, nearly spitting out the words.

Ronny and Len had had enough. They pushed their way through the group who started up their chants and shouts again. Ronny and Len scowled at them.

Pauline had got up from her stool and had begun to realise for the first time that all was not well. This group of people actually did not like the minstrels. Did not like them? How could anybody not like them? She was confused.

As they were talking, though, Pauline eased herself round to be at the stage door. She held out the envelope with the rose inside it as Ronny came towards her. She smiled and said: 'I wasn't expecting to see you so early, Ronny. Here's your rose.'

Ronny Wilkinson took one glance at Pauline, then ignored her and swept into the theatre, with Len Suffolk close behind.

Now there was a buzz of activity. The reporter was busy jotting down in his notebook. The photographer was pleased with the picture of the scowling Ronny he had just taken.

Pauline, quite unperturbed at the slight she had just received from her hero, was more baffled by the response to the show that would be going on in a few hours' time. She approached the leader of the protest group and tapped her on the shoulder.

'Excuse me,' said Pauline, 'but I don't understand. I saw the Black and White Minstrels 568 times at the Victoria Palace and nobody ever complained. I'm wondering why it was never wrong then, but it's wrong now. What's the difference?' She looked up into Julie's face with complete innocence.

Someone else was confused by the commotion. The Mayor, Harry Graham, had just left the conference hall and his address and lunch reception for the W.I. ladies. His chauffeur was now driving him past the stage door and he could see instantly what was going on. Upon spotting the Deputy Mayor, he asked his driver to stop the car.

Mayor Graham took off his chain of office, got out and went quickly across the road. The Deputy Mayor saw him and withdrew from the group to meet him.

'What the hell's going on, Jim?' asked Harry Graham.

'Some of us felt strongly enough about this show to discourage them from coming here again,' replied the Deputy Mayor confidently.

'So you started a protest, at council level, without advising me!'

The Deputy Mayor had no difficulty in maintaining his calm.

'Sure, Harry. We didn't want to bother you with this one,' he said with a warm smile.

Harry Graham looked him straight in the eye.

'Why not?'

The Deputy Mayor began to lose his composure for the first time.

'Well, er, you have quite enough to do, Harry. We didn't want to bother you.'

'Didn't you, Jim? Well, it's a great pity you didn't consult me first. You see, when my parents brought me over here from Jamaica in the sixties, the Black and White Minstrels was the first show I ever saw on television. I liked it, all those songs and the dancing. And I'll tell you this. I've booked two tickets for my wife and me for tonight's show. And we're going to go along for a damned good time.'

The Mayor waited for no response but went straight back to his car.

The young reporter, who had sidled up to the pair unnoticed, could not believe his luck. His tongue toured his lips over and over as he wrote down verbatim the disagreement he had just heard between the Mayor and his deputy.

Pauline was the first to regain her composure before anybody on the scene and she settled back on her stool.

'He'll be out soon for a cup of tea across the road,' she confided to herself. 'I'll be able to have one with him. I'll give him his rose then. That's what I'll do.'

Backfire

Harry pounded on, working his way up the Gulf Coast. Only 3000 paving stones to go! Running was such a bore to him out here. It was so featureless. He was glad of this stretch though, even if it did make Canvey Island look like north Cornwall.

Harry looked out across the Gulf as he ran and breathed in the sea, even though the air was hot. Running in his native Yorkshire was so bracing compared with this territory. One, two, one, two. The sea was so still. The Arabian Gulf; he wondered anew why he had to call it that. Ever since schooldays he had known it as the Persian Gulf. His students always got uptight if he referred to it that way. One, two, one, two. Heading north, Kuwait in the distance, two hundred and fifty miles away. Oops, that was another thing. He ought to think in kilometres. Never mind. When these thoughts go in a minute, work out exactly what two hundred and fifty miles is in kilometres. One, two, one, two.

Now, what was it about Kuwait? Something this week. Talks broke down between them and Iraq. That was it. Oh well, par for the course in the Arab world. Daresay a few more months'll go by and they'll talk again. One, two, one, two. How many paving stones left? Oh, God. Why is the terrain so uninteresting? It's either concrete or stony desert. No variation. Now then, what's two hundred and fifty miles in kilometres?

Twenty minutes after working it out he reached the company compound. He met Dick and George running to it from the other direction.

'Don't know why you didn't rest up this morning,' shouted Dick. 'Man of your years ought to be saving hisself for this afternoon.' His friend laughed.

'Oh, I'll give an account of myself,' protested Harry. 'I know

97

I can't get to your standard. But at my age I'm no longer bothered about winning.'

'Just as well,' laughed George. 'These morning runs are getting a bit sticky now, aren't they?'

'I'm surprised we're getting away with it this much,' replied Harry. 'Last summer was far more humid than this.'

'I wasn't here then,' observed Dick. 'But you still have to get out early these days.'

'It's six o'clock now,' agreed George. 'Another hour and it would be unbearable.'

'What time's the race?' asked Dick. They were walking towards the reception area of their compound.

'Starts at five,' answered Harry. 'The heat should have died down by then.'

'That's if it starts at all,' said Dick as they went through the doors, 'what with the emergency.'

'What emergency?' asked Harry.

'Didn't you catch the World Service before your run?' George responded as they collected their keys.

'Well, there's no other move we can make at present,' said Don Bartlett to his deputy. 'We've got all the maintenance crew in on twelve-hour shifts from six o'clock this morning. We're on indefinite alert.'

'That's very good, sir. I'm sure you've done the right thing,' said Benton.

The area manager looked at his wall map. 'We'll certainly please the Saudis, taking such firm initiative. And that's what it's all about, isn't it, Peter?' He smiled and looked Benton in the eye.

'I'd say so, sir.'

'So what about all this?' Bartlett studied the wall map. 'He's already taken Kuwait City. Only a matter of time before he reaches the border.'

'Will he stay there though?' queried Benton thoughtfully. 'What if he goes into the neutral zone between us and Kuwait?'

Bartlett stared blankly at Benton. 'Well, if he does that, we'll have to discuss with London about evacuating the wives and children.'

'Hm. Won't the Saudis see that as a panic move?'

98

'We'll have to consider that, of course. Mustn't do anything to risk losing the contract.'

'No, of course not, sir,' echoed Benton. 'What about this afternoon?'

'What about it?' Bartlett spoke abstractedly as he was still studying the map.

'The big race,' Benton reminded him.

'Oh, the half marathon,' remembered Bartlett. 'Of course. Oh, well, yes, we'll have to go ahead with it. Annual event. First Thursday in August. We must keep everything as normal. The one thing we mustn't do is to let the Saudis think we're getting rattled.'

'I quite agree, sir.'

There was a babble of noise in the compound dining room where they were now serving lunch. The three men hovered around George's transistor radio.

'Iraqi forces have now surrounded the British and American Embassies,' declared the crackled voice of the newsreader, 'after attacking Kuwait at two o'clock this morning and quickly taking command of the airport.'

'Poor sods,' exclaimed Dick. 'They've got hostages now. Masses of them.'

Harry looked gloomy. 'Well, I reckon that's put paid to my plans. The wife was due out here in a fortnight. I'm certainly not bringing her out to a war zone.' He gave his attention back to the radio.

'The United Nations Security Council put down a Motion this morning condemning Saddam Hussein's action and it was passed by fourteen votes to none, with no abstentions.'

'Fat lot of good they'll do,' declared Dick. 'The United Nations is useless.'

'Yes, their record isn't good, is it?' observed George. 'Wonder what they'll do this time.'

'That is the end of the news,' the sound waves produced. 'Now here is a message from the Foreign and Commonwealth Office. Anyone planning a visit to Kuwait is advised not to travel there under any circumstances. Any British citizen living in Kuwait is advised to stay in his own home. That is the end of the announcement from the Foreign. . . .'

Harry switched off the radio. There was silence between the three men for a few moments.

'God, what must their thoughts be now?' said Dick gloomily. 'There are still several families from my time out there. No chance to escape. Not enough warning.'

'Wonder where *we* all stand in this,' said George. 'Saddam could come down here along the coast road easy as anything; all this oil down here.'

'I reckon the oil'll save us,' put in Harry. 'I can't see George Bush leaving this place alone.'

He looked at his friends. He could see he had not convinced them any more than he had convinced himself.

Dick picked up the newspaper on the table. It was two days old.

'Well, it's certainly put Ian Gow's murder in the shade,' he said, as he scanned the headline.

'Yeah. Wicked bastards,' declared George. 'They want stringing up, like Saddam.'

At which point another race competitor came to them to say that the event was definitely on.

'Not many people about, sir,' observed Benton.

'Typical,' declared Bartlett. 'If we put this on in work time, they'd all flock to it to get away from duties. But because it's a Saturday, I mean Thursday, ha ha, still confuse the weekend days out here, they just don't want to know.'

'Not like the services, eh, sir?' sniffed Benton.

'Damned right, Peter. Twenty years in the RAF. Never once asked for anyone's agreement. They just did it. And God help them if they didn't obey.'

'Quite so, sir. They don't know how lucky they are out here. Especially the teachers.'

'Oh God, don't talk to me about the Teaching Unit. Have more trouble with them than anyone. Poofy bunch of liberals. Always asking "Why?" '

'Always remember my old C.O. saying to me once that the rule he'd always followed was to have complete faith in his superiors.'

'And he was absolutely right, Peter. Because you see, if you

100

don't have complete faith in your superiors, you don't have a chance of winning a war.'

Benton nodded approvingly.

'Now then,' said Bartlett. 'Let's see if we can get this thing started.'

They walked towards the starting line. There was a straggle of some thirty competitors, roughly half British, half Saudi.

'Well, Abdullah,' said Harry to the young man standing next to him. 'What do you think of your chances?'

'I have good chance,' laughed Abdullah. 'I train very hard this week.'

'Only this week?' asked Harry. 'That's no good. You've got to get out there every night. Always.'

'Oh no,' protested Abdullah. 'This very hot country. I am don't run every night.'

'Ah well, you'll pay for it this afternoon,' said Harry, slapping Abdullah on the shoulder.

'Right, gentlemen,' shouted Benton, 'will you all take your positions, please?'

They stopped milling around and quietened down. One or two of the fathers looked across at their proud children watching from the sidelines. Because of religious custom, none of the mothers had been allowed on to the base, so the children were commanded to be on their best behaviour.

'You know the rules,' said Benton. 'Three times round the circuit finishing at the shed over there.' He pointed vaguely and they all looked in the general direction. 'You'll be directed all the way along.'

The men jostled into some sort of formation. The majority were only doing it for a laugh, just for the sake of something to do, and the spectators stopped talking about the Iraqi invasion for a few seconds to pay attention.

'Right, sir,' said Benton to his chief. 'They're all ready.'

'All correct on parade are they, ha ha?' said Bartlett, unaware that nobody was joining in with his good humour, except Benton who coloured a little.

'Right, gentlemen.' Bartlett cleared his throat. 'I'll just say "On your marks; go".'

He raised his voice on 'Go', and one or two of the Saudi competitors who were looking confused immediately set off.

'No, no, not yet, chaps,' Bartlett called out. 'I was merely telling you what I *would* say.'

The Arabs looked even more confused but returned to the starting line.

Harry rolled his eyes upwards at Dick.

'All right, we'll try again,' said Bartlett. 'On your marks.'

They poised themselves.

'Go.'

The Arabs sped off, to a man, as if shot from a cannon. Dick, George and Harry moved off at a slower pace and laughed.

'Do this every year,' said Harry. 'They never learn about pacing.'

Soon the runners were out of sight. One or two of the children ran after them, taken by the momentum of the occasion, but soon returned. Bartlett and Benton took a slow stroll through the row of date palms towards the path near the shed.

'Well, they got away pretty smartly,' observed Bartlett.

'Yes, sir,' Benton echoed. 'Good to see all the Saudis way out in front.'

'Indeed, Peter. It might all work out for us.'

Benton looked at his chief. 'I do hope so. I've been thinking; it could look quite awkward for us if we have to pursue our plan.'

'How do you mean?' Bartlett asked nonchalantly.

'Well, the spectators,' Benton replied.

'Oh, we don't have to worry about them. They'd understand perfectly in the circumstances, or if they don't, too bad.'

'I'm not thinking about the Brits,' Benton persisted. 'What would the Arabs think?'

Bartlett looked around him. 'Can you see any Saudi spectators about?'

'Well, no,' replied Benton.

'And nor are we likely to get any,' said the confident Bartlett.

'Yes, but they might hear about it.'

'If they do, they'll keep quiet. They're the last to say anything that puts them at a disadvantage. You know what face savers they are.' Bartlett guffawed.

'I hope you're right, sir,' said his deputy.

'Don't worry about it, Peter.'

The three British runners were slowly gathering ground past a number of Saudis. By the time they circled the sports stadium, several had dropped out altogether. As the route wound round towards the barracks, two other Brits decided they had also had enough. One collapsed by the barracks entrance.

'Are you OK, Phil?' Dick said as he came upon him.

The other man waved and tried to smile, too exhausted to speak.

Dick ran on, George by his side. 'Can't think why he does something like this,' he said. 'He never trains.'

'Daft bugger,' observed George. 'He'll kill himself one day. You all right, Harry?' He turned to the man running on the other side of him.

'Fine,' said Harry. He refused to say more, to conserve his energy. They were just approaching the shed for the first time.

'Winning post is somewhere here, isn't it?' panted George.

'Yes, I think we go down that path to the right of it,' answered Dick as a cheer went up from the small crowd standing there. Bartlett and Benton smiled and nodded. 'They'll direct us, I expect,' continued Dick.

They made the lengthy circuit a second time and now, when they reached the barracks entrance, a small group of Saudi air cadets emerged to see what was going on. There were not many of them as the majority had left for the weekend. They cheered the Arabs still left in the race and laughed at Harry, unable to believe that someone as old as he would run a long race.

And indeed it was Harry's age that took the edge off his performance. By the time they reached the shed again, a gap was opening between him and Dick and George. The latter two were keeping up a strong pace and were clearly in front. A cheer went up at the shed, but the smiles had somehow disappeared from the faces of Bartlett and Benton.

The two leaders ploughed into the third lap. About another ten minutes and it would be all over. Harry saw the gap widening between himself and his compatriots. Then he found himself overtaken by Abdullah Al Qatani who had declared earlier that he had 'good chance'. Ah well, youth was bound to get the better of him, Harry reflected. Not to worry. He was still determined to have a go.

Dick and George ran almost jauntily past the stadium. One of them looked back and could only vaguely see one competitor in the distance. Their lead was now a commanding one. After circling the stadium they came upon the barracks for the third time. George was glad it was the last. He was beginning to tire in the late afternoon heat. The air cadets standing at the entrance could not bring themselves to cheer, as the leaders were not Saudis.

Dick and George swung round the last corner and could see Bartlett and Benton in the distance. Bartlett was waving a small flag and gesturing towards the righthand side of the shed. They came closer. George realised he would have to let Dick go ahead to win. He just did not have the energy left to maintain the effort.

Following the direction, Dick ran towards the shed then veered to the right of it. A few people applauded as Bartlett indicated the table positioned conspicuously on the open ground beyond.

Dick came to a stop, stood astride and bent forward. George was not long after him and threw himself on the ground outstretched. Bartlett and Benton came over to them.

'Well done, chaps. Excellent race.'

Dick and George nodded and panted hard. Dick hoisted himself on to the table. George remained on the ground.

Bartlett smiled. 'Hope you didn't mind about the diversion.'

Dick blinked at him uncomprehendingly. 'What diversion?'

Bartlett said, 'You've done this race before, haven't you?'

'No,' answered Dick. 'Neither of us was here last year.'

'Oh, I see,' said Bartlett. He turned to Benton, handing him the flag. 'There you are, Peter. You know where the official finishing line is.'

Benton took the flag hurriedly and beat a grateful retreat.

'What are you talking about: a diversion?' Dick persisted and by this time both he and George were on their feet facing Bartlett. The area manager was already rattled. He resented all attempts at being spoken to with even a hint of insubordination in the voice. Yet he could not do anything about it. He was no longer in charge of servicemen.

'It's very simple,' said Bartlett, trying very hard to be casual. 'It was thought that in the circumstances it would look better if a Saudi won the race.'

Two mouths dropped a mile each.

'You what?' exclaimed George incredulously.

Bartlett cleared his throat. 'We have a potentially serious situation brewing in the Middle East with this morning's news. We must do everything to keep the Saudis feeling on top. Kuwait is only two hundred and fifty miles away after all.'

'So you thought that to keep the Saudis sweet we must have them winning this race?' Dick was wide eyed.

'It was a joint decision,' protested Bartlett.

'Don't give us that crap,' said Dick angrily. 'This is all your doing. We've been here long enough to see how much you kow-tow to the Arabs.'

'Don't you speak to me like that.' Barlett's nostrils were flaring. 'Some of you people don't realise the situation. All right. It was entirely my decision, and one based on the £10 billion contract this company holds with the Saudis. Don't forget part of that goes towards your high salaries.'

'And your possible knighthood,' muttered Dick.

'What was that?' demanded Bartlett.

'Nothing,' replied the accuser. 'So what about the Saudis? Don't you give them any intelligence for seeing what you've done?'

'They'll only see the result,' proclaimed Bartlett. 'That'll be good enough for them.'

Dick and George turned away in disgust.

Harry turned the corner by the barracks. All he saw in front of him was Abdullah. Logic told him that he could not possibly win the race. Dick and George had gone on ahead some time before. But he did think he might catch up with Abdullah who seemed to be flagging after that last spurt.

Making his greatest effort, Harry gave it all he had left and gradually gained ground on Abdullah. As he came nearer he could see Benton holding the flag up and looking perplexed for some reason. But Harry's concentration was set upon Abdullah

Al Qatani and it was with supreme satisfaction that Harry just managed to overtake him in time and reach Benton's falling flag before Abdullah.

Harry recovered quickly, turned around, elated, and still could not work out why Benton was looking so confused. He noticed that Bartlett had just come on the scene and was looking even worse. Harry quickly forgot them as he went back to Abdullah who came across to give him a hug.

'You right,' laughed Abdullah. 'I must train more.'